THE GRINCH MAKES GOOD
Alison Kent

Harlequin Books

TORONTO • NEW YORK • LONDON
AMSTERDAM • PARIS • SYDNEY • HAMBURG
STOCKHOLM • ATHENS • TOKYO • MILAN
MADRID • WARSAW • BUDAPEST • AUCKLAND

For Friends

To the ones on-line I made this year and who found their
way into the pages of this book, especially Steven Bailey
and Doug Peters. To the ones in real time of whom I wish
to always be worthy, especially Jan Freed, Annette John,
Marian May, Jolie Kramer. To my best friend, the very
patient Walt Stone, on-line and in real time, for reasons he
alone needs to know.

ISBN 0-373-25764-3

THE GRINCH MAKES GOOD

Copyright © 1997 by Mica Kelch.

What is happening here?
Brooke asked herself

"Isn't it obvious?" Duncan asked and answered at once, pressing the front of his body into the back of hers.

She'd spoken aloud! "Yes," she managed to say. "And it has to stop."

"Why?" he asked, splaying one hand on her stomach.

She wanted his touch higher. She wanted his touch lower. She sighed. "We're standing in the lobby." She almost added, *And you're a grinch who doesn't believe in Christmas.*

"No one's here. It's dark." His lips settled against her nape. "And we're standing under the mistletoe." His hand moved. Boldly. Upward. Covered her breast. Her breath deserted her. "What do you want, Brooke?" Duncan asked.

She wanted relief. Release. She *needed* him to believe in Christmas. "Duncan, we can't do this."

He let her go and she turned to look into his eyes. There was a riot of confused emotion that she sensed came from whatever had happened to make him a grinch.

"Just kiss me, Brooke. That's all. Please."

Their lips met tenderly, with tentative movements and slow exploration. Then he stepped back and touched a finger to her face, shaking his head. Before he walked away, he reached up and slapped at the mistletoe as if it were a pesky mosquito.

Dear Reader,

I love Christmas.

My without-a-doubt, to-die-for, absolute favorite time of the year. But I live in Southwest Texas, which fairly guarantees I will not have a white one.

What can be guaranteed is that I'll have a tree that stays up entirely too long, another Santa or two or three to add to my collection and an abundance of good food (read: chocolate) and fun.

Writing the character of Brooke Bailey was the best type of fun. Vicarious fun. Through Brooke, I was able to do all the decorating and entertaining I never seem to squeeze into my real life. I also had the opportunity to give myself the best present of all—Duncan Cox. After all, don't we as women, as homemakers and mothers and professionals, deserve a hero?

Yours sincerely,
Alison Kent

P.S. I love to hear from readers. You can write me at Harlequin Enterprises Ltd., 225 Duncan Mill Road, Don Mills, Ontario Canada M3B 3K9.

Books by Alison Kent

HARLEQUIN TEMPTATION
594—CALL ME
623—THE HEARTBREAK KID

1

"MEN. Bah, humbug."

Brooke Bailey lifted the tip of her calligraphy pen from the burgundy velvet cuff of the Christmas stocking and grinned. Leave it to Sally White to twist Dickens to suit herself.

"Now, Sal. It can't be that bad, can it?"

"Of course not. It can be worse." Sally punctuated her statement with a very long, very Sally sigh. Coming to the bottom of the staircase, she stepped into the lobby of the apartment building she and Brooke shared with their elderly landlady and six other young, upwardly mobile professionals.

From her seat on the hardwood floor, Brooke followed the other woman's progress across the Victorian-style room, which really was beginning to look a lot like Christmas. The common area on the first floor of the four-story walk-up had required but a fraction of the time she spent each year decorating her parents' home for the holidays.

And that left her more time for, well...she counted at least a dozen projects that would keep her busy for the next twelve days. Maybe this wouldn't be such a bad year after all. This first Christmas ever away from home. This first Christmas spent with friends instead of family.

She capped her pen, looked up and mulled over Sally's expression, then stated the obvious. "He canceled."

"Yes, he canceled." Sally paused in front of the Christmas tree, blocking the sparkle of the tiny white electric candles reflected in the pink and gold antique balls. "Being stood up for a date I could handle. But this was business. A potential client."

"Not to mention an enormous coup for White Publicity. Which means you'll reschedule as soon as possible," Brooke added, though Sally hardly needed the reminder.

Four years living across the hall from the blond bombshell had taught Brooke more than she'd thought there was to know about determination. Persistence. Tenacity.

Any of the traits could have gained Sally status as an honorary Bailey. She'd certainly make a better one than Brooke did at times.

"Of course I'll reschedule." Sally began to pace, her steps a staccato echo in the small room. "I told Dr. Howard I'd call first thing Monday. Lord, Brooke. Do you know what it would mean to the agency to sign Mercy Hospital?"

Oh, Brooke knew exactly. More hours for a friend who already slept less than six hours a night a week and devoted the remaining eighteen each day to business, except on weekends. "Exhaustion?"

"I won't have time to be exhausted," Sally said.

"You won't have time for anything. Forget that personal life you're so fond of." Having a personal life was not a high priority for most of the career-driven people Brooke had known, her parents included.

But then, this was Sally. Sally loved her personal life, and actually had one. One worth bragging about. Lucky wench. Brooke made a face. "Of course you know I'm kidding."

"Of course I know you're kidding. We both know my personal life is the only thing that keeps me sane." Sally smiled the same smile that had convinced Brooke four years ago she'd made a friend for life.

"I'm not sure your sanity-retention plan is working," Brooke said to same friend. "Otherwise, why would you even consider taking on Mercy Hospital as a client with the schedule you already have?"

"That's easy," Sally answered. "I love what I do. Which is the exact same reason you're able to turn a store the size of Fielding-Lane into a Christmas showpiece even though it requires months of meticulous planning."

She stopped her pacing and glanced from the Christmas tree to the row of hanging stockings, to the freshly lettered cuff of the one drying on the seat of the deacon's bench Brooke was using for a table.

"At least I leave my work at the office," Sally said, lifting one brow.

The expression was one of concern, not accusation. Brooke knew that, knew her friend's interest was genuine, a true indication of Sally's caring nature.

"Since when?" Brooke countered. "Besides, this isn't

work. This is Christmas. I love Christmas." More than she was going to admit to Sally. Or to anyone.

It seemed a bit silly to be *this* sentimental. This attached to a season. But even though she wouldn't make the admission, neither would she deny the wealth of all that Christmas made her feel.

"I love Christmas, too," Sally said, fingering the delicate gold chain at her neck. "But that doesn't mean I'd spend my Saturday morning decorating this lobby."

"And no one would expect you to," Brooke returned, the corner of her mouth hinting at a wry smile. "But if Santa was here, you'd be advising him which stop on his world tour to make first for most impact."

"Ah, touché." Her brown eyes sparkling, Sally made her way across the room to where Brooke sat. "And if you ever see me bringing work home, remind me of this conversation."

"That'll be tough to do since I'm usually asleep by the time you drag in from the office—" she arched both brows "—with reams of paperwork tucked under both arms, no doubt. I can barely hear your front door from my bedroom, you know."

"You listen for my front door?"

"I do when it gets late and I know you're not home. Not that I worry. I just...worry." Brooke thought of Sally as family. A bit of worry wasn't out of order.

But listening for Sally didn't make her crazy. Oh, no. That came in the morning when she waited for the running of the shower in the apartment upstairs. It always came minutes after she stepped out of her own and turned down the music she played to help her shake off the remnants of sleep.

It had become the strangest habit, listening for the early morning footsteps, the creak of the wood flooring, the squeal of hot water through stubborn pipes. Stranger that she heard the shift of body weight from tile to porcelain, the slide of metal rings over the shower-curtain rod.

The latter part she imagined. A ridiculous imagining, really, thinking of Duncan Cox stepping into his shower. She barely knew the man. He'd lived above her for only one month. Long enough for her to realize that the hours he kept were not to her liking.

Not that his comings and goings disturbed her. He was quiet. Except for the shower. And most of that distraction was in her own mind. No, what disturbed her was that he worked incessantly and she found him attractive regardless. She knew better.

"You're sweet to worry," Sally was saying. She added a light sigh, "And you're right. If I get the Mercy account, something is going to have to give. And it's certainly not going to be my personal life."

"I thought as much." Shaking off thoughts of Duncan Cox she had no business thinking, Brooke removed the finished stocking from the deacon's bench and handed it to her friend. "Honestly, when I think of all the men you go out with, I don't see how you keep up."

"Easy," Sally answered, gingerly holding the stocking between forefinger and thumb. A saucy grin lit her face. "I use a spreadsheet."

That comment coming from anybody else would have given Brooke pause. As it was, she didn't spare a second thought. "A spreadsheet. Hmm. An idea so obviously calculated it slipped right by my right brain."

"It's simple organization. Horizontal rows. Vertical columns. Headers. The usual." Stocking in hand, Sally crossed the small lobby to the wainscoted alcove opposite the building's front door. "Though lately I've found very little data to input."

"Dating data. What a concept."

"One whose effectiveness is in direct correlation to the variables at hand."

Brooke nodded automatically. "You mean it's useless."

"Exactly. I obviously need to change my approach to this man thing." Sally placed the stocking just so on one of the brass hooks set into the wall-*cum*-faux fireplace before returning to Brooke's side. "I think I'll start dating alphabetically. Where's the phone book?"

Brooke sputtered tea across her lettering stand. *Shoot*, she thought, blotting the drops with a tissue, knowing the mess was exactly what she deserved for teasing her friend. "Sorry. I choked on the leap from spreadsheet to phone book."

"I'm kidding, of course. Though if I get desperate, remind me I thought of it." Inclining her head in Brooke's direction, Sally smoothed down her form-fitting winter-white sweater dress and perched the barest edge of her bottom on the clean end of the bench. Three-inch cream-and-brown stilettos gave her stunning legs even more stunning length. "You almost through with those?"

"Last one," Brooke said, uncapping her pen to letter the final stocking.

"Good. I'm starving. And don't give me that look that says you've changed your mind. You promised me Saturday brunch. It's Saturday. And time for brunch."

"I'm not dressed for brunch," Brooke hedged, knowing that her black leggings and hip-length red, cashmere sweater would work as well as Sally's more...Sally attire. Brooke straightened her legs and wiggled her toes. The antlers on her reindeer slippers bobbed rhythmically. "See? No shoes."

Sally raised her gaze from Brooke's feet to her face. "Brooke, hon. We need to talk."

"No we don't," Brooke said, and laughed. What had she ever done without Sally in her life? She set about lettering her own name in gold script on the burgundy stocking cuff. "What we need is to eat. If you'll run down to La Madeleine, I'll buy. That way I won't have to change shoes."

"The fact that you don't want to change shoes is what worries me."

Brooke frowned, turned her ankles this way and that. "They're not that bad, are they?"

Sally started to slowly nod, then switched directions and shook her head. "As long as you don't wear them tomorrow night to the reception. Which was a great idea, by the way."

"Thanks. I think so, too. And I promise to ditch the

slippers...but only because they clash with the Victorian theme of the room." Brooke grinned at her friend's pained expression, then made a visual sweep of her decorating efforts. "You don't think the lobby's too small, do you?"

Sally brushed off the question. "For what you have planned it's perfect. Informal as well as intimate."

"Informal. Exactly." But intimate? That word brought to mind the shower upstairs. The picture of sleek wet skin. Spikes of damp hair. And steam, smelling of soap and Duncan, drifting into the space between his floor and her ceiling to sweeten the air of her bathroom below.

She blew out a shaky breath. Then inhaled to regain her control. Duncan was the consummate workaholic. That put him off-limits. Way off-limits. The beat of her heart told her so.

"I don't want to make a big deal out of it. There's only nine of us. Just thought it would be nice for everyone in the building to have a chance to get together."

"And most of us are staying in town for Christmas. It's like our own little family." Sally reached for the finished stocking. "Are you and JJ going out tonight?"

Brooke hung the stocking loop on Sally's outstretched finger, wishing she could blame the sudden knot in her stomach on hunger. Or even on the vision of a wet and naked Duncan Cox. But this was a different tension. A troublesome one. Because soon, very soon, she was going to have to deal with the issue of J. J. Mackey. "We did Thai food last night," she said.

"And that precludes you from going out tonight?"

What precluded her from going out was the fact that JJ was getting too serious too fast. And that as much as she enjoyed his friendship, there could never be more. She didn't want more. Not from JJ.

Brooke shook her head. "I promised Nettie short-bread cookies. It's Saturday. Bunco."

Sally tilted her head to the side, swung the stocking on her finger and sighed. "Don't you find it strange that you're thirty-one and single and spending the official thirty-one-and-single night of the week baking cookies instead of exploring the possibilities with that most gorgeous specimen, J. J. Mackey, M.D.?"

"No stranger than you, at thirty-one and single, having plans to spend the same night of the week at a business dinner instead of exploring gorgeous possibilities of your own," Brooke answered, returning her calligraphy pens to their case and disassembling and storing the lettering stand.

"We are some pair," Sally said, and got to her feet.

While Sally hung the final stocking, Brooke took a last look around the room. Gilded grapevine garlands tucked with sprigs of green holly and pine wound their way up the staircase banister and trimmed the jambs of the first-floor doors. Lace snowflakes and bows tied in mauve and ivory satin moire decorated the lush, ten-foot blue spruce she'd dragged the stock boy through the Christmas tree lot to find. Of course, she'd tipped him well.

Individual stockings, each with a resident's name scripted in gold calligraphy, hung waist level from the oak wainscoting on the lobby walls. The decor was simple enough. Certainly not Martha Stewart perfection. But it would do just fine.

Brooke was sorry she hadn't thought of dressing the apartment lobby before this year. Sure, she'd gone home to Dallas the last three Christmases. But not everyone living in Nettie's place had a home to go to, the finances to travel or the time free from work.

That was the case with Sally this year. Her public relations agency had taken on several clients with seasonal needs. Sally doubted she'd spend more than a few hours with her parents on Christmas Day. The rest of the Whites understood, of course. Were supportive, of course. There would always be another Christmas, after all.

Well, that's where they were wrong. So very wrong.

Brooke took a deep breath and looked at her friend. Her gorgeous friend. Her ambitious friend. Her successful, driven, enterprising friend. And she said, "You know, Sal, you and JJ ought to get together."

Sally's head whipped around. Her platinum blond curls followed, a delicious froth that danced around the startled expression on her face. Outrageous or outraged, Brooke couldn't tell for sure. Perhaps a genuine mix of both. The thought had come out of nowhere, but the more she considered it, the more sense it made.

Sally opened her mouth. Closed it. Opened it again. "You're kidding me, right?"

"Not kidding at all," Brooke said, then turned back to load paint pens, calligraphy stand and rolled plastic sheeting into her tote bag before settling down in one corner of the deacon's bench with her tea.

Making a slow, thoughtful trip across the room, Sally eased down onto the opposite end of the bench. Arms crossed beneath her breasts, she turned a contemplative look Brooke's direction. "I thought you and JJ—"

"We're friends," Brooke supplied. "He's a great guy. Funny. Endearing. Ambitious and aggressive. But I'm not what he needs. And vice versa."

Sally's expression softened into one of tender concern. Friendship. "What do you need then?"

"Me?" What *did* she need? Other than what everyone needed? To love and be loved? To belong? Boy, didn't *that* sound pathetic.

Brooke blamed the blip in her normally steady pattern of feelings on the time of year. And the fact that she wouldn't be going home for Christmas when she'd always gone home for Christmas. There wouldn't be Christmas in the Bailey household now that Nanna was gone.

The end of a tradition wasn't the end of the world. Rationally, Brooke accepted the change. Emotionally, she switched gears.

"What do I need? I was thinking along the lines of a long vacation. Blue water. Tall, fruity, tropical drinks with paper umbrellas. Cabana boys."

Like the intuitive friend she was, Sally took the bait. "Cabana boys and tropical drinks, huh? I was sure you were going to say babies and bottles and sweet-smelling powder—"

"Your biological clock must be ticking again for the idea to even cross your mind." Brooke eyed Sally teasingly. The game was a running one—Sally's denial even while she oohed and cooed over every baby she saw.

"My biological clock is digital. No sound."

"Is that so?" Brooke sipped the last of her tea, thinking that her own clock should have been ticking loudly. It wasn't, though, and she couldn't help wondering if it ever would.

"Very so." Sally cocked her head and appeared to listen. "Definitely no ticking. Though I do hear footsteps thundering up the front porch."

A half second later the glass-inset front door swung outward and Dr. J. J. Mackey walked through, followed by Dr. Duncan Cox. Brooke's stomach tumbled, tea and all.

She briefly took in JJ's sweat-stained T-shirt and running shorts before her gaze was drawn back to Duncan with his broad bare chest and gray sweats jaggedly slashed at the knees.

While JJ's fashionable sunglasses hung from his neck on a neon yellow cord, Duncan had left his dark shades in place. A black sports band creased his damp hair from ear to ear.

The hair on his head was a caramel brown, but now clung in short wet strands, glistening and dark. His chest chair was lighter, sprinkled sparsely in a wedge over slick, tempting skin. His coloring was that of a desert bird of prey.

Brooke felt the flutter of wings in her chest, a free-fall dive in her stomach. She couldn't help thinking of the shower, the water running above her, over him.

She inhaled a whimper and swore life wasn't fair. Swore she was going to move from this building after she'd finished up Fielding-Lane's spring solstice campaign. Or at least after Easter. Memorial Day?

Then she realized she was staring. And Duncan was staring back. His dark shades concealed his eyes, but she felt their impact anyway.

JJ flashed both killer dimples and used his hands to comb his damp hair. The black strands refused to obey, falling forward naturally into a look for which hairdressers charged mega bucks. "If it isn't Sal. And Brooke, her pal."

"First a doctor. Now a poet." Sally got to her feet, made a pitter-patter motion with her palm in the center of her chest. "Be still my heart."

Brooke looked from one to the other. A slow smile spread over her face. Yes. Definitely two of a kind. "You two need to take that act on the road."

"Act? I'm crushed." JJ slipped onto the seat next to Brooke and swung an arm over her shoulder.

She ducked away. "Keep your sweat off my sweater or you *will* be crushed."

"I love it when you talk sexy," JJ said, draping his arms along the back of the bench and stretching out his bare legs.

"And when would that have been?" Brooke teased, but only a smidgen. JJ's flirting was calculated and she knew exactly the bottom line he was aiming for. He wanted a trophy wife, a socially charming woman to add to his picture of success.

He brushed off her comeback as easily as he brushed

a lock of loose hair behind her ear, his fingertips lingering to drift down the sensitive skin below.

She smiled, sweetly she hoped, watching his eyes darken and wanting to deflect the heat. He was sexy and gorgeous and successful and not at all what she was looking for.

Not that she was really looking.

"You sure you can't make dinner tonight?" JJ asked. "I'd love the company."

"You'll have plenty of company. The entire board of trustees. And their wives. Who you'll no doubt charm senseless."

"I'd rather charm you."

"But I have way too much sense to let you." She pursed her lips. "At least most of the time."

He leaned to the side—her side. His lips, warm from his run and his natural body heat, grazed her ear. "I knew it. That kiss last night scrambled the ol' gray matter."

More like whipped it into a froth of confusion. Brooke got to her feet, blew out a shaky breath, then realized she and JJ had a rapt audience. Her ceramic mug slipped from her hand to the floor.

When she bent to retrieve the broken pieces, Duncan bent, too. He beat her, handed her the four shards of the cup and the handle, which had snapped off in one piece.

"Shoot," she mumbled, and thought *Nice hands*, noticing their veined strength for the first time as Duncan reached up to pull the sports shades from his head and tuck them into his pocket.

She cleared her throat, looked into the coffee-and-cocoa-colored eyes she'd felt on her earlier. "And thanks."

He nodded, stood as she did, continued to hold her gaze.

Look away, Brooke. But his lips moved. So she looked directly at his mouth. At his lips. And wondered. If he enjoyed kissing. In the shower.

"Did you know you have antlers on your feet?" he asked.

The ultimate humiliation. She waited for the floor to open up and swallow her. Didn't happen. Funny how she hadn't been bothered a bit while buying the slippers with JJ.

Ah, well.

"Not only that," she said, digging the hole deeper and sliding up the hem of one leg of her leggings, "I have a partridge in a pear tree on both ankles."

"Socks?" His mouth quirked a tad. "For the twelve days of Christmas?"

She nodded and bit down on the admission that she had on matching panties. "Today is December 14. The first day of Christmas. At least according to the way I've worked out the song, which probably isn't true to legend."

The look in his eyes was an interesting one, a bird-of-prey sort of searching quality. The eyes looked away, then back. "Twelve days until Christmas. Six more until New Year's. Another eighteen days of insanity. Whaddaya think, JJ?'' Duncan turned to his friend. "How many emergencies will have holiday madness written all over 'em?''

JJ got to his feet, swiped his sweat towel over the back of his neck. "Way more than I wanna think about.''

"Yep. Ya gotta love that spiked eggnog mixed with the Christmas blues.''

"Enough shop talk, Dr. Grinch,'' Sally said to Duncan as she stepped between the two men, crossed her arms and glared at first one, then the other. "Brooke is doing her best to make sure we all have a Merry Christmas.''

Duncan looked from Sally to Brooke. "Some of us prefer our Christmas straight up. Without the merry.''

Brooke was still back on the eggnog and the blues and had to refocus. Surely she hadn't heard what she'd just heard. "No stockings hung by the chimney with care? No chestnuts roasting on an open fire?''

Duncan shook his head deliberately.

He couldn't be serious. "Not even Dasher, Dancer, Prancer or Vixen?''

"Dancer, Prancer and Vixen.'' JJ frowned, but the effect was as false as it came. Dimples tended to do that. "Isn't that the trio you treated with penicillin and condoms at the clinic last week, Duncan?''

"Oh, very nice, JJ,'' Brooke grumbled, biting back a grin. JJ needed even less encouragement than Sally.

Which was one more reason they would make a perfect match.

Brooke turned to Duncan then. "Well, do your best to enjoy the holidays. And don't let my efforts persuade you otherwise."

"I won't." He propped his fists at his lean waist. "But thanks anyway."

She needed to let it go, but was truly curious. "Won't do your best? Or won't enjoy them?"

"I won't enjoy them." He pulled off his sweatband, shoved it into the pocket of his shorts with his shades.

"How do you know? It's only December 14."

"Trust me. I know."

Hmm. He'd yet to witness even a scaled-down version of Brooke's Bash. If her celebrations could bring together the bullheaded Baileys, one recalcitrant emergency-room doctor would be a piece of cake.

Her determination kicked in. She knew it would show in the set of her mouth. "Don't be too sure."

"That won't happen."

Brooke frowned thoughtfully. He wasn't too sure at all. He was just right sure. His confidence was a perfect fit.

So was his incredibly fit body.

No. That thought hadn't come from her head, had it? Surely she had more class than to ogle bare shoulders and a bare chest and an elastic waistband riding low on a flat stomach.

Uh-oh. She was ogling. "Then as confident as you are that you won't enjoy the holidays, I'm equally confident you will."

"That's right," Sally said. "You haven't seen Brooke in action."

Duncan's eyes narrowed. "You don't say."

"I do say." Sally wrapped an arm around Brooke's shoulder.

Brooke glanced sideways at her loyal friend, patted Sally's hand and said, "Christmas at the Baileys' is more of a tradition than *It's A Wonderful Life*."

"More of a tradition than cookies left out for Santa," Sally added, stepping away from Brooke and into Duncan's face. "More of a tradition than—"

"I don't believe in traditions," Duncan interrupted. "Especially one steeped in commercialism. And misery."

Brooke knew of the misery he saw on the job. Wondered if there was more. "And I suppose you quit believing in Santa Claus before your fifth birthday?"

"No. I believed. Then." The tight set of his bare shoulders, the grip of his fist on the sweat towel he held, the hard set of his jaw... Yes, she wondered about the misery.

How could she not? Especially at this time of year. When for as long as she could remember her goal had been to dispel the bad feelings in all around her.

Hmm. Had she found a new goal for this year? Or rather a more specific goal than providing happy holidays for her neighbors? She needed time to think. To plot. To plan.

She needed to have her head examined. Had she forgotten about the shower upstairs? She dropped the broken mug remnants down among the art supplies in her bag, slung it over her shoulder. "I've got to get busy."

Sally followed her toward the staircase. "Let me grab my purse, then I'll run pick up brunch."

"Brunch?" JJ's blue eyes sparkled.

Brooke sent Sally a warning look over her shoulder, but it was way too late.

"La Madeleine, to be exact. What can I get for the two of you?" Sally asked, her gaze moving from JJ to Duncan and studiously avoiding meeting Brooke's as both men gave their order. "Great. We can eat and watch Brooke bake cookies."

"The shortbread cookies? The ones you made for Halloween?" JJ asked, moving closer.

"And Thanksgiving," Sally oh-so-thoughtfully added. "You two run upstairs and wash off the grit. We'll meet at Brooke's at noon."

A conspiracy. No way around it.

Brooke was already going to be rushed with the cookies after so much time spent on the stockings this morning.

Listening to Sally could be accomplished with one ear. Brooke had done it often enough. JJ didn't require much more attention. He could have her other ear.

But Duncan.

She blew out a long breath and started the climb to the second floor.

How was she going to bake and frost cookies, listen

to Sally and JJ, and do it all with the distraction of Duncan Cox in her apartment?

Especially when she couldn't shake the image of his shower upstairs, the impact of his coffee-cocoa eyes.

Men. Bah, humbug.

2

"WOMEN. Ya gotta love 'em."

Not necessarily, Duncan mentally countered, walking through his apartment's large, living-dining area and into the kitchen beyond.

JJ sat before the computer taking up half the space on the new dining table. Duncan spared him a brief glance, frowning at the picture the setup made.

He really ought to buy a desk for the bedroom and get the system out of here, he thought, tossing the towel he'd scrubbed over his damp hair onto the kitchen countertop. But then again, maybe not. He kind of liked things the way they were.

He didn't mind the navy blue towel on the white tile, his worn, brown deck shoes shoved up against the laundry room's accordion door, the computer sitting exactly where it didn't belong. Each gave a semblance of controlled clutter in a life where chaos ran amok.

The women he'd known would've badgered and huffed about the mess. Not to mention the hours he kept, the way his job came first. The way he needed to stay involved with the masses who benefited from his commitment to his career, instead of devoting his time to one special woman.

No. JJ was wrong. Duncan didn't have to love 'em at all.

"Look at Brooke." JJ rambled on, oblivious to Duncan's thoughts, cruising from one internet chat room to another. "Here she is for the first time in her life spending Christmas away from home. And what is she doing?"

Duncan snagged a bottle of water from the fridge, screwed off the top and slipped his bare feet into the deck shoes. He wondered why Brooke wasn't going home. He wondered, but that was all. "Making a pest of herself?"

JJ shook his head, the physical reaction indifferent. Unconcerned. "No. She's making cookies. The ones from Halloween."

Funny. No response to the pest comment at all. JJ wasn't usually so detached from his passions. Duncan tossed the bottle top in the trash. "I wasn't here at Halloween."

"That's right." JJ grinned, eyes still focused on the scrolling computer screen. "You still hadn't returned from the great Northwest. Man, how *did* you do it? I would've molded inside a month. I don't know how you kept sane enough to become Seattle's golden boy with so much water, water everywhere."

Duncan had been able to do what he'd done because he'd kept busy. Kept involved. Growing a reputation while growing older. Growing impatient.

"Yeah. Well, I'm back now. And the only mold around here is in the fridge."

"I see your sense of humor hasn't suffered the same

fate as your ambition, my friend," JJ finished, logging out of the internet service and turning Duncan's way.

Standing in the arched opening between kitchen and dining area, Duncan tipped the water bottle to his lips, drank deep, then said, "I'm the same guy who ambitiously ran down your scrawny quarterback butt in varsity practice."

"Was that before or after you ate my dust in the fourforty?" JJ cocked back in the dining chair, hands behind his head, one foot squared over the opposite knee.

"I let you win and you know it. I always let you win," Duncan replied, the familiar battle a comfortable one. A smile pulled at his lips. He gave in, relaxed enough to lean back against the kitchen archway.

"Right." JJ nodded. "You always let me win. Which would explain the way you bloodied my nose over that sweet little pigtailed Jenny Hiller in third grade."

The water bottle popped in Duncan's hand. He eased his grip. Marginally. "I had other things on my mind in third grade."

"Let me guess. Miss Collins. The goddess who taught us reading, writing and 'rithmetic." A short laugh punctuated JJ's thoughts. "Was there a boy in class who didn't spend at least half that year in serious prepubescent love?"

"I doubt it." JJ was right. Miss Collins *had* been on Duncan's mind. But not like she'd been on his friend's.

No, Duncan had spent third grade wondering if his teacher would ever compare the signatures on his permission slips to the ones on his report card. She never had, and by fourth grade he'd become a master forger.

By fifth grade he was master of himself.

"Well, whatever, I'm glad you're here." JJ slapped one palm on the table and got to his feet, slipping his hands into the pockets of his khaki Dockers. "Now to get you out of ER and back into a practice to rival the one you had in Seattle."

Duncan stepped aside to let his friend into the kitchen. "Not a chance. I came here to do exactly what I'm doing."

Emergency was just the sort of nonstop madness that made him tick. It put him where he was needed, where he didn't have time for distractions...like reindeer slippers and partridge-in-a-pear-tree socks.

"You're crazy, you know. With your reputation, your talent." JJ gave a disgusted shake of his head and jerked open the refrigerator door.

Duncan headed into the living area, needing the breathing room before this argument got going again, as it had repeatedly throughout the month he'd been back in Houston. "My talents are not going to waste. Trust me on this."

"The issue isn't whether or not you're wasting them, but how they're being used. I just don't see how you can settle for the hours and the caseload and the tension of emergency when you could obviously have more."

"More than what? More than I know what to do with?" One thing that had certainly never been a problem, he thought, plopping down on the tufted blue sofa and propping both feet, ankles crossed, on the coffee table.

JJ stood in the kitchen archway, screwing the top from his water bottle. "Mercy's board is eager for new blood. For doers, ready and needing to get involved. You're exactly what they're looking for. You're hungry."

"Not as hungry as you." Duncan leveled the mouth of his water bottle in JJ's direction.

JJ shrugged. "Our appetites lie along different paths. And it's a very good thing."

"Good thing for who?"

"For us, of course. Cuts down on competition when we're not going after the same things. But it's also good for the hospital." JJ took hold of the top rung of the dining chair he'd sat in earlier, spun it and straddled it in reverse. "Do you have a clue of the changes we can make?"

Duncan did. But he wasn't quite sure his and JJ's methods were simpatico. JJ was all politics. Duncan dug in the dirt. Which, now that he thought about it, could have easily described his friend's get-ahead methods as well.

Thing was, Duncan's dirt came from hard work, not hardball. "I have more than a clue. And I'm making my changes. In emergency."

JJ spent a couple of seconds studying the water bottle in his hand. Then he sighed and a grin broke out on his mouth. "You know, our differences are a good thing for the women, too."

Hmm. "Which women?"

"All women."

"Ah, thought you had a particular two—" or even a particular one "—in mind."

"Brooke and Sally?" JJ took a long drink. "Those two are a pair. Funny thing, but beneath all that fluff, Sal's a shark. And I mean that as a compliment. She's got that go-for-the-throat drive."

"Sounds like just your type."

"Nah. We'd rip each other to shreds...not that the idea doesn't hold a certain appeal," JJ added as an afterthought.

Interesting. And unexpected. "Thought you were interested in Brooke."

"I am."

"Ah, you're trying to sell *me* on Sally's charms." Which were not at all unattractive.

"And why not?" JJ lifted both brows. "She possesses great charms. And a very nice set of wits. Not to mention a hell of a brain."

This was getting weirder by the minute. Duncan really didn't want to get mixed up with JJ's women. Still, charms or not, wits or not, brains or not, Sally didn't have half the attitude that came with reindeer slippers and partridge-in-a-pear-tree socks.

Neither did she have raven black hair that should have looked coolly severe when pulled back into the tail Brooke usually wore low on her nape, but instead looked warm and inviting, like silk waiting to slide through his fingers.

Or eyes that sharp shade of blue that saw more than a man wanted to reveal. Intelligent eyes. Perceptive eyes. Eyes too keenly focused below the surface to the heart.

Or a body that made a man think of the texture of a woman's skin, the feel of her curves in his palms, the give of her muscles beneath the press of his fingers. The sheen and dampness of her arousal.

Damn.

"The thing is," JJ was saying, when Duncan shook off Brooke's bold image, "Sal's charms at times are a bit outrageous. But you take Brooke—her perfect composure, her professionalism—and voilà."

Perfect composure. JJ obviously hadn't looked close enough into Brooke's eyes. There was a look there, a look about her, what she saw... "Right. Voilà. The exemplary Mrs. Dr. J. J. Mackey."

Pushing to his feet, JJ crossed the room and slumped back in the overstuffed chair set at an angle to the couch. He sighed as he settled. "Convincing her of that has not been the piece of cake I thought."

Duncan couldn't hold back the edge of a smile. "The ol' Mackey charm deserted you, eh?"

"Only when it comes to Brooke Bailey."

That brought a strange jolt. His smile faded. "So give it up already."

"You're kidding, right?"

"Wrong. If it's not working, move on. She's obviously *not* the exemplary Mrs. Dr."

"Ah, but she is. Elegant. Sophisticated."

Right. Reindeer slippers. Partridge-in-a-pear-tree socks. Elegant and sophisticated. "Two requirements that would be right up there at the top of my list."

"I didn't know you had a list."

"I don't. But if I did I'd be looking for a lot more than elegant and sophisticated." Which were only two of the qualities he saw in Brooke Bailey.

He could admit to seeing more, but wouldn't. Because what he saw in her he refused to dwell on and had ever since he'd moved into the apartment house a month ago and realized JJ had staked a claim. Duncan might mess with his childhood friend when it came to sports, to careers, but never when it came to women.

Especially when any messing he did with Brooke Bailey wouldn't have been serious, anyway. She wasn't his type. Not that he had a type. Or was even looking to figure out what his type might've been.

But neither was Brooke a woman to mess with just for fun. Which was all he had time for these days.

"Well, obviously that's not all. She's incredibly successful. Have you walked through Fielding-Lane's lately?" JJ sat forward in the chair as his excitement grew. "I swear the store rivals Neiman's. Amazing what she pulls off. Especially at Christmas.

"She's looking to take over the art direction for the entire Southwest region. That's fifteen stores, Duncan." He reached up, ran a hand over his hair. "She's dedicated, creative, ambitious...."

Duncan got the picture. "And she would reflect well on you."

JJ looked up sharply. Seemed to honestly consider Duncan's statement. "If you look at it that way. Sure, that's gotta be a part of it."

At least the man was honest. Duncan gave him that. "I don't look at it any way at all."

"Good. Because I need objective advice."

"About?"

"Brooke, dammit."

Duncan wasn't sure he wanted the advisory position. For some reason the term "conflict of interest" came to mind when there was absolutely no reason it should have.

"What about her?"

Elbows on knees, JJ swirled the contents of the water bottle he held in one hand. He studied the spinning liquid a moment, then admitted, "Nothing's working. C'mon, Duncan. You saw her earlier. The way she backed away."

Yeah. He had. "What exactly was I seeing?"

"We go out. We have a great time. But when it comes to my career? Like the board dinner tonight? No way. She won't have a thing to do with it."

The crux of the matter. Duncan set the water bottle on the table, crossed his hands behind his head and tried to decide which way to go. "Maybe you should take that as a sign."

JJ slumped back. "Yeah. A sign that I need to take a different approach here. My usual charming methods aren't working worth squat."

"Whoa. A Mackey? Admitting failure?"

"Failure? I don't think so."

"Well, it couldn't be a cry for help," Duncan stated, realizing it was exactly that. He'd known JJ a lifetime. And he owed him a lot.

"Crying isn't exactly my style. And it's not help I need as much as...direction."

"This must be where my advice comes in."

"Yeah. You got any?"

"About women?" He shook his head, took a drink from his bottle. "Nope. Don't know a thing."

JJ snorted. "Right. You can pull that wool over one of the guys upstairs. But not me. Don't forget, I know twenty-seven years' worth of your secrets."

"You think I've let you in on all my secrets? You don't know anything but what I've told you." The shake of JJ's head said Duncan was full of it. And he was. But he'd also accomplished his mission, so he went on. "Let's just say what I know isn't what you need to help with this problem."

"That's right. You're too serious about work to be serious about women."

"Depends on your idea of serious." He wasn't getting serious, no. Didn't mean he couldn't. He just had other things to be serious about. The clinic, for one thing. Staying involved. Giving his all to the less fortunate who needed what he had to offer.

"Serious as in there is no Mrs. Dr. in your future."

That was true enough. Not that the idea didn't hold a certain appeal. It was just that it would never work.

He hadn't met the woman yet who understood his priorities. Instead they wanted to change him. To get him to cut back on his hours. To give up his causes.

To make him enjoy Christmas.

It wasn't going to happen. He owed himself that much honesty at least. Owed himself more. The admission that this had always been his worst time of year. Now more than any other time he had to stay on track, to keep busy, to make sure Christmas didn't get in his way.

To make sure reindeer slippers and partridge-in-a-pear-tree socks didn't trip him up.

He had to get the image out of his mind. And now. He had to quit thinking about what wasn't his type. What he couldn't have. What he'd sworn to steer clear of. He tuned out his own thoughts and realized JJ was talking about a Christmas gift for Brooke.

"She isn't the roses type," JJ said.

"No, she's not," Duncan remarked in offhanded agreement, thinking if she were any type it would be long-stemmed, exotic, one-of-a-kind.

"And chocolates aren't really her style."

Unless the chocolate was heated and drizzling off the tip of a strawberry onto her skin.

"She doesn't wear a lot of jewelry."

She didn't need to. Not at the hollow of her throat, or at the underside of her wrist. Not on her delicately long fingers, the purely female lobes of her ears.

"So, I'm at a loss."

And Duncan was going insane. "Try a household appliance."

"Right. And get an even colder cold shoulder."

He pushed to his feet, headed back to the kitchen and this time reached for a beer. "Hell, JJ. Not all women like the flowers, candy, jewelry routine. What does Brooke like? You said she's elegant and sophisticated, right?"

"And ambitious and creative and dedicated."

"Yeah. You mentioned those, too." What he hadn't mentioned was sexy as hell. Which was probably for the best.

Duncan was in no mood right now to think about sex. Not in connection with a woman his best friend had his eye on. And not with his December frustration level higher than ever this year.

He was certain that had a lot to do with his return to Houston and the eventuality of running into his parents. But he could do a lot of good here. And so he was staying.

He might need to find a new apartment. One with more tenants. A larger number of faces to see on a daily basis, rather than just the nine who lived here. Then he wouldn't be as likely to so often run into the one whose apartment was directly beneath his.

The one who ran her shower every morning at five. Who played sultry female singers just low enough to make him strain to hear above the rush of water. Who sang along, her voice off-key, pitched low, so throaty and intimate he set his alarm even on the mornings he needed to sleep in.

The one he pictured wet. Her black hair slicked back by water and by hands with sensible short nails and the need to touch. She'd done it earlier—patted Sally's hand. She did it with their landlady, Nettie May, hugging the older woman, placing a palm on her back.

He imagined those hands on his chest, water pounding down his back, soapsuds lathered in a pool at her feet, steam swallowing their bodies. Her touch. Arousing him.

Comforting him. Fingers working the troubles of the day from his neck and shoulders. Drifting over his skin in a touch that was nothing more than simple, necessary human contact.

The appeal of her nurturing was as frightening as it was a mighty need. As powerful as desire.

And that juxtaposition of thoughts was a hell of a way to start the day. If not a bit voyeuristic. He swilled a long draw from the bottle of beer and stayed where he was in the dark kitchen. Tried to refocus on JJ's problem. To distance himself from the intimacy and redirect his thoughts.

"So be creative. Make an impression."

"I'm only creative when it comes to noses and chins and the occasional breast." One knee crooked over the side of the chair, the other leg stretched straight, JJ turned to look behind him, in Duncan's direction.

"I don't think a gift of cosmetic surgery will get me very far. Besides, there's not a thing on Brooke that needs changing."

Duncan agreed. Physically, she had an exotic look, dark hair against light skin, strikingly bright eyes, a mouth that he couldn't help but watch when she talked. She was the look of his fantasy. And she would look damn good in his shower. "I wouldn't go that far."

"Name something."

"For one thing, she could keep her Christmas cheer to herself instead of involving all of us," Duncan groused, not the least bit apologetic, either. To JJ. Or to himself.

He'd seen his name on one of the stockings on the wall. Hanging right there with the rest of them. As if there might actually be something in it on Christmas morning.

He was too old for stockings. And fairy tales.

JJ was silent for a minute, then retorted, "Ah, Dr. Grinch. Still hung up about Christmas, I see. Thought you might've gotten over that by now."

Duncan really wasn't in the mood for this now. Or ever. "Gotten over it since when? Since you saw me this time last year?"

"Last year you were in Seattle. By yourself."

"Where I am makes no difference." He shrugged, for no one's benefit but his own. "I still see the same things."

"The same things you see day in and day out." This time JJ got to his feet and circled around to prop a hip against the back of the plump chair. He crushed the empty bottle in his hand before he spoke.

When he did, his voice was low. "Not every case that walks through emergency during December has to do with Christmas, Duncan."

"Enough of them do."

"Enough for what?" JJ looked up sharply, his eyes lit with that inner fire that had driven him to success. "Enough to make it impossible for you to enjoy the holidays? C'mon. You weren't a doctor in high school. You didn't like Christmas then, either."

"I was in a state of teenage angst."

"That doesn't explain third grade."

Duncan was silent, wondering what can of worms he'd opened by coming home. "Third grade was a long time ago, JJ. Let's leave it there."

JJ's sigh was consenting, but one that said he had not given up. "Not a problem."

"Good." Peace. At least for the time being. "Besides, you already have one problem on your hands."

"Brooke? She's not a problem."

Duncan paused in the kitchen archway, lifted a brow. "Then what are we talking about here?"

"Okay." JJ shifted to the other hip. "A bit of a problem. But nothing I can't handle."

"So you don't want my advice."

"Did I say that?"

"Make up your mind. I would've thought you'd had your fill of fumbling back in high school. On the field and off." He lifted the beer to his lips to hide his smile.

"I haven't dropped a ball since. And I don't intend to now."

"What *do* you intend to do?"

"I thought you were going to give me the benefit of your years and experience."

"Seems like we've been through this...." Duncan let the spoken thought trail off, pushed away from the kitchen archway and made his way into the dining area.

"What we have here is the collective genius of great minds at work."

Perched on the corner of the dining table, Duncan

shook his head. "Never thought I'd be part of a think tank to figure out women."

"Not women. Just Brooke."

They really had to get beyond Brooke. So they could get beyond brunch. And cookies. Duncan had to be at the clinic at five, though heading there now held a certain escapist appeal.

He said the first thing that came to mind. "She obviously likes Christmas."

"That's a serious understatement."

"So, do something for Christmas."

"I'd planned to."

"No. I don't mean a gift."

JJ headed for the kitchen, returned with his own beer. "Don't give her a gift?"

"Of course, give her a gift. That's not what I'm talking about."

"Then what?"

Why was this so hard? Why was he even involved? *Easy, Duncan. This is JJ And that's all the reason you need.* "Women get sentimental over the silliest things. Simple things."

"I should give her something simple, silly and sentimental."

"Damn, JJ. If I could spell it out for you I would, and save us both the hassle, but I can't. It's that thing that puts that look in a woman's eyes." He pushed to his feet, paced toward the kitchen.

"That look."

"Yeah. You know the one."

"The one that says 'oh baby baby'? Or 'I want to

have your baby'? Or the one that says 'if you call me baby again I'm gonna knock the crap out of you'?"

Duncan laughed. "No. The one your mother got that last weekend before she took the bar exam. When your dad corraled you and me and your sisters and packed us off to Galveston for the weekend." That look had stayed with Duncan. A long time.

The way Carolyn Mackey's eyes had glistened with a mixture of relief and gratitude and love. It was an emotion that Duncan, at ten, hadn't known what to make of. That Duncan, at thirty-five, still thought about.

"Ah," JJ said. "That look. And Christmas should do it."

"Anything that means something to Brooke should do it."

"Okay. I got it." JJ looked panicked. "Got a suggestion?"

At this point, Duncan realized he might as well do this himself. "I see you're still having trouble thinking on your feet."

"My only serious character flaw. I'm a strategist, not a spur-of-the-moment kinda guy, which is why I'm a plastic surgeon." JJ lifted his chin in a bogus cock-of-the-walk showdown. "I'm not crazy enough to tackle emergency medicine."

"Well, we all have our crosses to bear," Duncan said, and glanced at the dining table, behind the computer, at the basket of ornately wrapped exotic fruits his parents had sent him as a welcome home.

He grabbed up the large pear wrapped in white

webbing and lace stenciled with a bird of ruffled plumage and tossed it to JJ. "Here. A pear. With a partridge. For the first day of Christmas."

The light dawned. "The twelve days. Why didn't I think of it?"

"You would have if you only had a brain."

"I have one. See how I just used it to get you to solve my problem?" Smug and satisfied, JJ bounced the pear in his palm, flicked a finger at the feather attached to the stem. "I can take this to brunch. You ready?"

"No."

"You're not ready?"

Duncan shook his head. "I mean, no, don't take it to brunch. Surprise her. When she'll least expect it."

"You think so?"

"C'mon. What woman do you know that doesn't like a surprise? Especially if she's not sure who it's from."

"Wait. Back up." JJ gestured with the beer bottle he still held in the other hand. "Don't tell her it's from me? Doesn't that defeat the purpose of this exercise?"

"What purpose is that? Giving her pleasure? Gaining her gratitude?"

JJ appeared to seriously weigh the options offered: "You're right."

"Of course I'm right. I'm the doctor, remember?"

"And what does that make me?"

"The one with the problem," Duncan answered, then drained his beer. He headed for the kitchen one last time.

"Not really. My problem is solved. As soon as we figure out the next eleven days."

We? Duncan tossed his bottle in the trash. No, dealing with Brooke was up to JJ. She would never be Duncan's problem. Never. "Why don't *you* get this day out of the way first? Then work on number two tomorrow."

Frowning, JJ carried his own empty beer bottle to the trash. "Two turtle doves. Then French hens. Four calling birds. We're looking at a lot of fowl here."

"You don't have to be so literal," Duncan said, snagging his keys and wallet from the bar. "Use a little imagination. If you have that much."

"I'm sure I can handle it. I've made it this far, haven't I?"

"You know, her stocking would be the perfect place to leave that," Duncan said, nodding toward the fancy fruit JJ held. "The perfect place for all twelve, as a matter of fact."

"Means they'd all need to be small."

"Yeah, and we all know how much size matters." That drew the appropriate snicker from his friend, and Duncan went on. "Besides, think of the anticipation factor, the buildup. Make it a mind game."

"Mental foreplay?"

The next-to-the-best kind. "Unless that's too spur-of-the-moment for you. I mean, you could plan out this entire seduction in advance. Might spoil the fun of discovery, but, hey, it's your call."

A wide smile spread over JJ's face. "Let's go to

brunch, Dr. Cox. But first, a quick stop in the lobby to play Santa."

Duncan followed JJ out the front door and down the third-floor stairs, wondering how he'd gotten himself into this mess when he wasn't the one with the problem.

Women. No. He didn't have to love 'em at all.

3

MEN. Never in a million years would she figure them out.

Brooke stared into her bathroom's exaggerated hourglass mirror, expecting, at the very least, to see flour dusted across the bridge of her nose. Or drops of decorative green icing drizzled down the front of her red sweater.

But no. Nothing. The reflection showed only the black Holstein spots she'd sponged on the white wall behind, the lime green and grape Lucite accessories and the same nondescript female image she saw every morning.

Black hair with a blue sheen. Blue eyes with black circles beneath. At least she'd managed to color coordinate her face as well as her bathroom. She blew a puff of breath upward. Stray hairs sifted down and she tucked them into the band at her nape.

Ah, well. Whatever thoughts were going through the minds of the men in her kitchen weren't her problem. She didn't even have time to be curious. Though, of course, a part of her was. And rightly so.

One doctor couldn't stifle his cat-that-swallowed-the-canary smile. The other had refused to meet her eyes when they talked.

Come to think of it, she and Duncan *hadn't* talked. Not directly. The lunch-hour conversation had flowed around her while she worked, dividing dough into batches to roll and cut, coloring both red and green icing, washing utensils.

She'd added bits and pieces when her input was needed, but JJ and Sally had carried most of the dialogue, a rousing discussion of hospital politics and the world—Sally's world—of public relations.

Duncan had seemed more interested in the cookies than anything. He'd stood in the living area, leaning an elbow against the bar that opened into the kitchen and snitching more than a couple when he thought Brooke wasn't looking, focusing his attention on the debate at the table when he knew she was.

If the way to a man's heart was truly through his stomach, Brooke figured Duncan was hooked. Of course, the adage failed to take into consideration the owner of said stomach.

Duncan wasn't interested. Any more than she was interested. He had taken refuge in the distraction of the cookie process the same way she had. She'd wanted to give JJ and Sally time to set off sparks. Duncan just wanted to avoid being dragged into their conversation. Strange for a man who put so much store in involvement.

How Brooke knew these things, she wasn't quite sure. But she did. The same way she knew he'd step into his shower each morning minutes after she stepped out of hers. The same way she knew, having known him a month, that he wasn't her type.

Not that she'd determined the particulars of her type, but it certainly wasn't a man who buried himself in his career to the exclusion of all else the way Duncan did. The way JJ did.

Though Duncan's obsession to his calling appeared to be less driven by a personal agenda than JJ's, it still hit too close to home. Her father had devoted his life to his career in law. Her mother to hers in corporate real estate.

Both of her parents still spent almost every waking hour tied up with work. That was a fact that would never change.

The only thing that had altered in the least from one year to the next was the strength of Brooke's determination to balance each facet of her life. The professional with the personal. Friends with family, even while the rest of the Baileys were determined to work themselves to death.

It had always been business first in the Bailey household. Even at Christmas, when Brooke had been forced to scramble for every toehold on her quest to establish a family tradition. She'd had to scramble harder for family participation.

Being the Bailey black sheep had never been easy. But family was family. The bond of belonging—and acceptance—strong. Secure. Infallible.

Until this year.

Enough, she admonished herself. Life went on. She would adapt. End of story and of any self-pity that managed to slip past her resolve.

Shaking off the thought, she reached for the cube of

green glycerin soap. Two more sheets of cookies to bake and frost and she'd be done. Plenty of time to get the goodies downstairs before the "girls" arrived for Saturday night bunco at Nettie's.

Brooke's landlady was the sweetest thing, an atypical eighty-year-old, thrilled with the comings and goings of her eight thirty-something tenants. Since Brooke had moved to Houston four years ago to take the post as director of visual merchandising at Fielding-Lane, Nettie had related repeatedly that having young people around kept the toll of eighty years at bay.

Brooke believed her. Knew that more than likely it also kept the older woman active. Productive. Feeling needed. She didn't think twice about involving herself in Nettie's life.

Nettie's enthusiasm, her joie de vivre, her sense of integrity and bull-by-the-horns attitude reminded Brooke of her grandmother, who had died unexpectedly earlier this year. The loss hadn't lessened and had, in fact, hit hard the last few weeks. Brooke sighed. The melancholia was easy to understand. This had been their time of year, hers and Nanna's.

Brooke's Bash, as Nanna dubbed the annual holiday get-together, had been family time, the one time of year Brooke managed to assemble all the Baileys under one roof. It had started out as an effort to make a family of the blood relatives that bore the Bailey name.

But it had become what she did for Nanna and herself. And this year Nanna was gone.

She shook off the despondency. Christmas would

come and go. Maybe not as usual. The celebration would be smaller, friends instead of family, but change was a good thing. The one thing she knew she could count on.

Smiling, Brooke dried her hands, hung the black towel on the purple Lucite bar and squared her shoulders. She was ready to return to the project at hand— and to the three people taking up way too much space in her apartment. She headed for the kitchen.

"By then I was eyeing the forks laid out on the table," Sally was saying when Brooke entered the room, "trying to decide whether the salad, dinner or dessert tongs would make the best weapon. And leave the least mess."

Brooke rolled her eyes and patted her friend's shoulder as she walked past the table where Sal sat opposite a laughing JJ and a faintly amused Duncan. The exact responses she would have predicted from both men.

JJ was easy to read. But when it came to Duncan, she shouldn't have been able to make predictions at all. That implied a familiarity they didn't share. His shower didn't count.

No matter how intimately acquainted her imagination had become with him, those mental images of his warm wet skin, sleek wet hair and spiky wet lashes were only that. Mental images. Ones that, at certain times, she had trouble remembering were only that.

Stepping into the kitchen, she pulled the mixing bowl of cookie dough from the fridge and shivered. A response to the cold metal in her hand, nothing more.

She turned her attention to her three friends sitting

at the table in the dining area of the apartment's main room. "Thanks for sharing, Sal. And I'm sure I don't even want to know what it was you were talking about."

Sally winked playfully. "That's probably a good idea. This way you can honestly testify that you were unaware of any premeditation on my part."

Brooke rolled half the remaining cookie dough onto the floured cutting surface. "Let's see if I have it right. 'No, Your Honor. No need for a rope. Sally White is incapable of premeditation. Most of the time she's incapable of making sense. Just ask her.'"

JJ laughed, laced his hands behind his head and cocked his chair back on two legs. He cocked his smile as well. Sally's direction. "I don't know, Brooke. I think Sal's too smart to hang herself."

Beaming, Sally leaned toward JJ and patted his knee. "I do so like the way you think."

Brooke looked from one to the other. She had never been more certain of her instincts. This was an opportunity too good to let pass.

"You need to think about making that act permanent. A two-man show. Or in your case, that would be a man-woman show, wouldn't it," she oh-so-casually remarked, mixing the last of the sugar and water for the cookie glaze.

"Man-woman? As in a couple?" Sally arched a warning brow. "Brooke, hon. You've been too long in the icing."

Brooke paused with a finger halfway to her mouth, caught Duncan's eye, shrugged, then licked the icing away and reached into her tin of cookie cutters. The banter between JJ and Sally tickled her and she couldn't help but smile.

The way Duncan's eyes had flared, then darkened as she drew her finger from her mouth didn't affect her at all.

Nope. Not at all.

She looked down at the cookie—the Valentine heart—she'd cut. *Hmm*, she thought, and stared. A distraction of this type wasn't a good sign when she was trying to convince herself that he didn't affect her.

She tossed the unusable dough back in the bowl, the cutter into the sink and tried to remember where the conversation had been so she could safely return to it. "So, Sal. Just for future reference, which tongs *do* leave the least mess?"

Sally's smile revealed definitive satisfaction. "I never had to find out. That particular client managed to hoist himself on his own petard, so to speak. The arguments he made to void the contract backfired, binding him further. End of my dilemma. And now—" she turned her full attention to JJ "—back to yours."

"A dilemma? JJ?" Brooke asked, looking at the back of Sally's head, lifting her gaze to JJ. "What did I miss?"

"Now I really *am* crushed," JJ said, and laughed. Too loudly. Too falsely.

The only clues Brooke needed. "Ah, the board dinner."

He nodded, returned his chair legs to the floor with

a muffled thump. "Exactly. The one you couldn't fit into your busy schedule."

Baking cookies did not cut it as "busy" with J. J. Mackey, Brooke knew. He had *standards*.

But it was almost four o'clock. The cocktail party started at seven and was an hour's drive north of town. There was no way she could have made it even if she'd wanted to.

She didn't want to because it wasn't fair to lead him on. His career drive left her uneasy. She knew so well where he was headed, what his life would be like ten, fifteen years from now, how his calling would become an obsession.

She didn't share those ambitions. Which was why she needed to be careful about sharing his time. And his kisses.

She sighed. "You know my schedule, JJ. There just never seem to be enough hours in a day."

"There are always enough hours for what's important." Though his expression remained good-natured, his voice took on a bit of an edge. "Simple matter of priorities."

"I agree," she said, for the first time sensing Duncan's regard and tense energy. Pushing back from the table, he got to his feet, moved again to stand on the opposite side of the bar, as if he needed a better seat to identify the players.

She couldn't figure out why. It wasn't like she presented a threat to his friend. Barring the need to act as JJ's second, Duncan had no motivation for this much interest.

If concerned, protective interest was what she saw.

If it wasn't...if it was more...if it was personal... Her stomach clenched and she forced it to relax. No. It couldn't be. It just couldn't be.

JJ shoved a hand through his hair. "I guess we all do what we have to do."

"Exactly," Brooke agreed, ignoring Duncan's intent gaze while reining in her wandering thoughts. "Your career is important. The board dinner *should* be a priority for you."

"Right. Like baking cookies is a priority for you."

The edge in JJ's voice had sharpened. Brooke eased her grip on the aluminum shape she held tightly, but not before creasing a snowman into her palm.

"C'mon, JJ. Today's baking has been on my schedule for weeks. It's Nettie's turn to host game night. And the reception is tomorrow evening. I have to get this done today. Now."

Scooting around in her chair, Sally raised both hands, one palm toward JJ, the other facing Brooke. She looked directly at Duncan. "You have a suggestion on how to handle this, Dr. Cox?"

He shoved his fists in his pockets, rocked back on his heels, met Sally's gaze before glancing in Brooke's direction. "Boxing gloves? Baseball bats?"

Brooke met Duncan eye-to-eye through the open space above the bar between kitchen and living area. "I thought I'd try the silent treatment. My favorite passive-aggressive approach."

"Hey, guys." JJ unsuccessfully fought a smile that

settled the nerves of everyone in the room. "It's not that bad. Besides, Brooke knows I'm teasing."

Teasing. Oh, yeah, sure. Teasing was *exactly* what Brooke would have called it. Good grief. "Nothing like a little animosity between friends, right, JJ?"

"Anything you say." He flashed both dimples—on purpose. "As long as we can kiss and make up."

She rolled her eyes and went back to cutting the dough. "Hopeless," she muttered under her breath.

Duncan reached over and snagged another cookie. She smacked the back of his hand with her wooden spoon. "Doubly hopeless."

"Face it, Brooke." Sally's gaze encompassed both JJ and Duncan before she gave Brooke that look all women know. "We're dealing with men here. Hopeless is a given."

"Ah, there's the logic I knew I was missing," Brooke replied, cutting her eyes back to Duncan as he stuffed his mouth and shrugged. No eight-year-old could have done it better—all innocent boyish charm. And, dammit, it worked.

"Nettie's going to have your hide if she's short on cookies. And don't think I won't tell her exactly where they went," she said, casting an accusing glance toward his stomach, then wishing she'd looked anyplace else. There was just something about Dockers that rode low on lean hips.

Duncan licked the last of the glaze from the ends of his fingers. "You think she'll believe you?"

His eyes held hers, hypnotic and hunting, preying like any bird worthy of the name.

"She'll believe anything I tell her," Brooke said. And Nettie had better not prove her wrong.

Crossing both forearms on the open bar, Duncan leaned forward, his expression intent and aware. "The two of you must be more than landlord and tenant if you can so easily sway her to your way of thinking."

She scowled playfully. "She's my friend. Which means I don't have to sway her to anything."

"I thought maybe with cookies like these—" he indicated the racks cooling on the countertop "—she'd offer to knock a couple of bucks off your rent."

Brooke pressed the tree-shaped cutter into the dough. "Please. This is nothing but the *proverbial goodness of my heart*. True friendships come with no expectations. But you know that. Just look at you and JJ."

He appeared to consider her comment while looking down at the cookie outlines etched into the slab of rolled dough. Then he asked, "No expectations? Not even loyalty? Or trust?"

She shook her head. "Those aren't expectations."

"What are they then?"

Brooke listened to JJ's and Sally's voices in the background, thought about her family. Their expectations. About her friends. The differences between the two. Complicated differences, yes. But simple ones as well.

Her family expected her to bake cookies. Her friends kept her company, shared the downtime, added bad jokes and laughter to the ingredients. Brooke stopped, pulled in a deep breath. She hadn't meant to get so philosophical. She'd only meant to give Duncan an intelligent response.

Funny how the thought process spawned questions of her own. Like who had benefited from the Christmases she'd provided the Baileys. And had she been the only one without expectations, the only one to enjoy the giving spirit of the holiday.

Slipping a spatula between the dough and the cutting board, she lifted the shapes onto a cookie sheet. "Loyalty and trust embody the concept of friendship. You can't separate them as you would ingredients. It's part of the comfort level that defines the relationship."

"Then a friend is automatically someone you can trust. Whose loyalty you never question?"

This time she took but a moment to think, less to answer. "A true friend, yes."

"Nettie is your friend."

She nodded, smiled. This last response came as naturally as breathing. "Nettie is a dear. Sally, too. I don't know what I'd do without either of them."

"And JJ?"

Though she didn't think Duncan was prying, the question still caused a bit of discomfort. Because she knew he and JJ were friends. Lifelong. And that said a lot about the two men in her apartment. "Yes. JJ, too."

She glanced from Duncan to JJ and Sally. Their collective expressions of focused absorption offered the distraction she desperately needed. Talk about true friends. *Always there when you need them,* she thought, and smiled to herself.

Sliding the cookie sheets into the oven, she said to Duncan, "Those two seem to be having a heated debate."

Duncan leaned forward to peer through the kitchen archway at the pair arguing across the table. "I think they've forgotten we're here."

He was right. JJ and Sally were totally engrossed. In the conversation. In one another. Brooke was struck with an idea too brilliant for words. "I know who JJ should take to the board dinner tonight."

"Sally," Duncan said.

"Yes?" Sally turned. JJ looked up, as well.

Brooke mentally ran through the best approach, but settled for the only one that made a sort of Sally sense. She turned to JJ. "I have the perfect solution to your dilemma."

He looked doubtful, hopelessly so. "You don't say."

"I do say." Brooke glanced at Duncan. He gave a go-ahead nod. So she went ahead. "Tonight is important to your future, right?"

He nodded.

"And no date would most likely be preferable to the wrong date, right?"

He nodded again. Added, "As always."

Brooke growled. "Enough with the sweet talk. Pay attention. You're missing the obvious here."

"And what obvious would that be?"

"That you have not only the *right* date but the ultimate date sitting in front of you."

JJ looked from Brooke to Sally. Sally looked from Brooke to JJ. Brooke rolled her eyes at the both of them and looked at Duncan. Duncan snagged another cookie and popped it into his mouth.

"I give up," Brooke said, and turned to set the oven timer.

Seconds later, JJ arched a brow Sally's direction. "You game?"

Sally tossed her curls and answered, "You just try to stop me."

"Finally. For a minute there I thought I might have to lead you two single file through the idea." Dusting her floury hands together, Brooke crossed her arms and faced her guests. "Are we all happy now? We all have plans for tonight?"

"All of us but Duncan," JJ said.

Duncan straightened, took a step back from the bar. "I have plans. I'm working at the clinic."

"Dancer, Prancer and Vixen again?"

"Funny, Jay," Duncan said, and JJ snickered.

"What time do you have to be there?" Sally asked.

Duncan checked his watch. "Not until five. Why?"

"Brooke will need help getting the cookies down to Nettie's."

Good thing Brooke loved her friend. Otherwise she might have had to hurt her. "I can manage, Sally. It's only one flight of stairs."

"But how many trips and how many trays?"

"I can manage, Sally," Brooke repeated, adding a dozen unspoken words with her eyes.

"It's all right," Duncan said with the enthusiasm of a condemned man. "I have time."

"Great," Sally said, totally ignoring Brooke's visual warning. "I'm going to drag JJ upstairs to his place and let him fill me in on the evening so I can whip up a strategy."

Brooke looked at her friend. "You're awesome when you're in action. Those board members won't know what hit 'em."

"Wrong. They'll know they've been hit. They just won't know how it happened. And they'll never again look at Dr. J. J. Mackey as just another pretty face."

JJ still didn't look totally convinced. "As long as they look at me."

"What I'm going to do for you will knock your socks off."

"You knock the board's socks off and I don't care if I end up butt naked."

Sally went into business mode. "Speaking of which, I need a tour of your closet. I think that's the best place to start."

"I've been dressing myself for quite a few years, Sal. I know what not to wear."

"Yes. But do you know what *to* wear?" She got to her feet. "Let's get moving. We have work to do and so does Brooke."

Brooke waved Sally back to her chair. "Oh, please. I'm fascinated."

JJ moved in behind Sally, took her arm. "We'll be back to fascinate you more another time."

"I can hardly wait."

JJ's smile was confident. "Duncan. Watch yourself at the clinic."

"I always do."

Brooke glanced from one man to the other. So similar in commitment and determination. Yet so different in fire and fight. They made for an interesting pair.

She accompanied JJ and Sally to the door. "I expect a full report tomorrow."

"I expect real brunch tomorrow," Sally said, then leaned forward to give Brooke a quick hug and added in a whisper, "I'll get him home early."

Brooke held Sally another second. She needed to clear the air. Now. "It's okay. He and I are just friends."

"You sure?" Sally mouthed, and Brooke nodded.

Sally stepped back and out the door. JJ followed, leaving with a "See you two later."

Brooke stared at the closed door and took a deep breath.

And then it hit her that she was alone in her apartment with Dr. Duncan Cox.

SALLY WALKED BY JJ's side up the flight of stairs between the second and third floor and down the hall to his apartment.

Two years. The period of time she'd known J. J. Mackey. A long enough period of time to have developed—at the least—a minimal level of comfort in his presence. Especially since she felt comfortable with clients she'd known less than two minutes.

So why did she feel like she was fourteen?

Sally White had never been fourteen. Never experienced teenage stomach flutters, never whispered to a best friend during a late-night phone call about her crush on "that fine guy in algebra."

She'd grown up fast, grown up hard, grown up facing unrealistic expectations. She'd been an adult child living with adult siblings accountable to adult parents. Not a normal childhood by anyone's standards.

So why now, right this very second, was her stomach fluttering?

The answer was so easy she couldn't help but smile. This was J. J. Mackey, whom she'd had a teenage crush on since he'd moved in on the floor above hers.

And because Brooke, who Sally knew held JJ's interest, had just given her the all clear.

What would a fourteen-year-old do now?

JJ fit his key in his lock, then pushed open the door to his apartment. His smile broke her heart. "I figure you know where the bedroom is. And the closet, for that matter."

Sally gave a flip nod, stepped into his living room. "Unless you talked Nettie into remodeling, I think I'll be able to find it just fine."

"She really did a great job with this place. I was amazed when I found it. Even more amazed when the apartment came up for Duncan. I can't believe anyone would voluntarily move outta here." JJ closed the door. Threw the dead bolt. Tossed his keys onto the bar.

Sally witnessed the male ritual. Witnessed and absorbed like a fourteen-year-old wanting the small memory for private times. "I don't think either of the vacancies were necessarily voluntary. More like cross-country transfers. You and Duncan just had serendipitous timing. The same thing happened with Brooke."

"You didn't know her before she moved here, right?"

"Why? Does it show?"

"No," he said over his shoulder as he led the way to the bedroom. "In fact, I'd guess the two of you have been friends as long as Duncan and I."

"Women don't necessarily make friends easier, but we do bond faster, it seems. Men's friendships are often forged over a lifetime. Women's in days. Brooke and I talk about everything."

He flipped on the light. Arched a brow. "Like men?"

She arched one in return. "Prying?"

"Nah. A late night and a long run this morning." He rubbed at a neck that appeared tense and taut, a neck Sally would like to have rubbed for him. Then he flashed his dimples. "I get obnoxious when tired."

"So I see," Sally teased. "I told Brooke earlier that I can't even afford the time to be exhausted."

JJ crossed his arms and leaned a shoulder against the closet frame. "Are you? Exhausted?"

She tried not to be overcome by the width of his shoulders. Swooning wasn't her style. "Only in the best sort of way."

"Satisfaction, right? Of a job well done?"

"Or of a job done to the most excellent standard. It's a feeling that feeds on itself."

"The more you accomplish the more you hunger for?"

"In a way, yes." She loved how they thought the same way. Even so, she needed to get this off her chest.

"I grasp at all opportunities. But I want you to know up front that's not what I'm doing tonight."

He frowned. "I don't get it."

"The business dinner that canceled on me for this evening? It was Dr. Howard." At JJ's raised eyebrow, she added, "I'm bidding on the Mercy Hospital account."

JJ was silent a moment, then answered, "Then tonight could be as beneficial to you as to me."

"Yes. It could. But that's not why I agreed to go with you. I want you to know that." It was important to her that he did for the obvious personal reasons she wouldn't share, but also for professional reasons. She valued her reputation, and even a compromise for personal gain was outside her ethical boundaries.

"I believe you," he said, and gave her a smile that almost made her come undone. Then he gestured toward the closet. "Well, don't just stand there. Have your way with me."

4

WOMEN. Never in a million years would he figure them out.

Duncan had felt a shift in Brooke the minute she closed the door. It wasn't a subtle shift, either. And her discomfort—not fear, exactly, though he couldn't quite put a finger on what it was—became more obvious the harder she tried to shake it off.

He stayed on the back side of the bar, giving her all the room she needed to avoid him. Which she would no doubt deny she was doing. It didn't matter what she denied, though. He'd seen subtler billboards.

How he recognized her denial when he hardly knew her he wasn't sure. But that didn't make the truth any less obvious. The same way he knew she'd thrown Sally at JJ for personal reasons as much as anything.

As intent as JJ was on winning Brooke, she appeared determined that it wasn't going to happen. At least not today. Because she had cookies to bake.

Yeah, sure. Cookies.

Women. Not a chance he'd ever figure them out. Hell, he didn't even want to try. And if he had, Brooke Bailey sure wouldn't be where he'd start.

"You really don't have to do this, you know."

He looked up, once again giving her his full attention. Not a hard thing to do. That black hair, a raven black with the blue sheen of the bird's feathers when hit by the right light... The way she sleeked it back and worried with stray hairs that to him didn't seem stray at all...

Hair that he wanted to see wet, in the shower—hers, his, either would work. As long as there was water and her hair was wet, slick, silky.

"I know," he finally said, because it seemed like the right response to whatever it was she'd said earlier. His response to the picture he'd just imagined pressed itself into the fly of his briefs.

A sudden bundle of nerves and energy, she busied herself looking for something to do in the kitchen. "I mean, you don't have to hang around here if you need to get to the clinic."

He shrugged. "I have the time. Unless you want me to leave."

Her smile was so shyly hesitant he couldn't believe it had stolen across her face. Not that a month of chance meetings on the stairs or at the mailboxes or the times spent listening to JJ ramble on had given Duncan great insight into her personality.

But *shy* and *hesitant* were two words he'd never have used to describe Brooke. That much about her he'd seen for himself.

"No. I mean, you're welcome to stay. It's just that this has to be fairly dull, watching me bake cookies." She laughed, and the sound grabbed hard at his gut. "I mean, *I* wouldn't want to watch me bake cookies."

Ah, but she wouldn't see the things *he* saw. The way

she measured ingredients with her eyes rather than with gadgets made him wonder if she could size up a man as accurately. And if she could, what would she think of him?

"That's understandable." He tried to ignore the way she chewed at her lip, but his stomach wouldn't let him. He wanted to feel the bite of those teeth. "I wouldn't want to watch *me* dig out a bullet from the gut of a sixteen-year-old kid."

She looked up slowly, her gaze focused and still, her hands the same. "Does that happen a lot?"

"Way too often," he said, his voice grim.

"And that's why you do what you do, isn't it?" she asked, fitting a padded mitt onto one hand. "The emergency room. Because things happen that shouldn't and you want to stop them from getting worse. If you can."

Funny that he found breathing difficult when there was no reason he should have. No reason at all. He and Brooke had never talked of what he did. Hell, they'd never had a real conversation. Until today. And still she saw what JJ hadn't, not even after knowing him a lifetime.

"Yeah. That's part of it. Not as glamorous as plastic surgery," he added. "Though JJ has reconstructed a few of the messes I've cleaned up."

"He's good at what he does."

She'd spoken in a statement, but he knew she'd asked a question so he answered, "Yes. He's very good."

"Will that help him get an appointment to the board? Or is that more of a political game?"

Bright. So very bright. And not afraid to tackle the issues. Another bit of the portrait JJ had left unpainted. Duncan wondered what else there might be to discover.

"It won't hurt, of course. In fact, Jay enjoys the political maneuvering so much, I wouldn't be surprised to see him give up his practice in a few years."

"And go into politics."

This time her assessment held no question at all. But her teeth caught again at her lower lip and he knew whatever it was she was thinking didn't come without a decision of sorts.

Damn, but JJ was in some kind of trouble, which was so par for the man's course Duncan had to smile.

He looked up as Brooke caught her breath, her expression cautiously awed. He couldn't help but question what it was she saw. Maybe she'd begun to take his measure. "I take it you're not a big fan of politics."

The oven timer buzzed and she took a minute to retrieve the pans of cookies before she answered. "Would it be politically incorrect to admit to a sort of ambivalence?"

"I wouldn't know politically correct from a political appointment. Which JJ can't fathom."

"Did he try to get you to go to the board dinner, too?"

Duncan watched her lift the cookies to a wire rack. "He's trying to push me down his yellow brick road. But tonight I think he was more interested in female companionship."

"Politically correct female companionship."

"Maybe," he answered. Again her statement was cut-and-dried. No question. No hesitation. No regret. And that intrigued him the most. "If that's the case, I'd say he picked the perfect date. Or you picked him the perfect date."

"That's because they're a perfect match. Both as driven as they come."

"And you're not."

"Driven?" She looked confident. Not pleased, particularly, but decisive in her opinion. "Aren't we all? In one way or another? Either driven to—" she fluttered a hand "—whatever. Or driven *by* the same."

"For example?"

She thought a minute, then settled on an answer. "Okay. An easy one. I'm driven to bake cookies by my affection for Nettie."

At least she hadn't said by the need to avoid JJ. Duncan wouldn't have liked that had it been the case. He was becoming more and more certain that it wasn't. "And you're driven to your affection for Nettie by..."

"How can you even ask that?" Her aim was off when she tossed her spatula into the sink. Either that or she was more than mildly aggravated at his question. She bent to pick up the utensil from where it had clattered to the floor and said, "Look at this place. What she does for us."

"Isn't that her responsibility? As a landlord?" He nodded toward the cookies. "You don't go to this much trouble for everyone who lives up to their responsibilities."

"No. I don't. But Nettle is special." Brooke leaned

back against the sink, toyed with the mitt she'd removed earlier. "She reminds me very much of my grandmother."

That wasn't what he'd expected. Judging from the bits and pieces of the day, she'd declined JJ's invitation for a frivolous afternoon of Christmas cookies. Or so Duncan had thought. This bit of humanity pleased him.

For JJ's sake.

"And you're driven to bring holiday cheer into this building by...?" He let the question trail off and waited.

She simply shrugged. "I love Christmas. Is that a crime?"

"Haven't checked the statutes lately, but I think you're free and clear." And for some reason obsessed with a day of the year that was nothing but a day of the year. Over in twenty-four hours like all the rest.

"I don't expect you to understand."

"I know that. And I don't."

"I know you don't. Just like I don't have to understand your resentment of the holiday."

"It's not resentment." What it was was so ingrained he was no longer sure he could analyze where it had started and when it had become a habit.

"Then what is it?"

He shrugged, then lied. "Apathy."

"Even apathy has a basis. Is it the commercialism?" she asked, then went on before he could answer. "Working in retail, I can understand that. This year, decorations at Fielding-Lane went up the weekend before Halloween." She shook her head in a sort of amazement. "It's what I'm paid to do, though, so I've learned to disassociate my own celebration from what goes on at the store."

"And you're able to do that?"

She seemed to consider. "I haven't really thought about it so specifically before, but yes. I can. I love what I do at the store, of course. But it's my job. What I do here is...my joy, for lack of better explanation."

"Joy. Is that what Christmas makes you feel?" he asked, thinking how he was no longer able to feel much at all when it came to the holiday.

When it came to anything, as a matter of fact. Yet it was strange how he was suddenly feeling that very lack of feeling.

He leaned his forearms on the bar, clenched both fists, then finally realized Brooke hadn't answered. And when he looked into her eyes, when that transparent blue innocence kicked him in the gut, he wasn't sure he wanted her to.

"It means a variety of things. To me it's always been home and family. Maybe I'm more sentimental than most. But none of us get to this point without a mixture of good and bad Christmases behind us. I'm lucky enough to say that most of mine have been good."

"JJ said you're not going home this year."

She gave a small shake of her head, reached for a bowl of icing and stirred the thin mixture before drizzling it across the cooled cookie tops. "Seems strange, too. I feel at loose ends."

The light dawned. "Maybe those loose ends are spearheading your Christmas cheer drive."

She smiled at that. "I suppose that's part of it."

"And the other part?" he asked, because JJ or no JJ, he enjoyed seeing her smile, wanted to see it again.

"I guess there is no other part." She laughed lightly.

He felt it keenly. Savored it deeply. And then she laughed a second time and he knew he had just lost his detachment.

"The loose ends are looser than I thought they would be," she admitted.

"Why aren't you going home?" A sane enough question.

"No reason to when no one else will be there." She finished one row of cookies, started on the next. "My parents have booked a Christmas cruise. My brother is skiing in Colorado with friends. My sister and her bunch are spending the holiday with her husband's family. And there you have it."

"What about your grandmother?"

Her movements slowed. The drizzle of icing from the end of the spoon dwindled to a drip. "She died. At Easter. This year."

"I'm sorry." It was such a pat response. He wanted to say more, but anything more personal would ring false. He didn't know her and had no intention of getting to know her.

"It's all right. She lived a wonderful life. It was unexpected. But these things happen. It was just her time, I guess." Brooke quickly finished the final row of cookies. "These will need a few minutes to cool before I can take them downstairs."

"I'm in no hurry." And he wasn't. Her expressions intrigued him. The way she fondly remembered her grandmother, sadly recalled her death. The way through it all she concentrated on the task at hand, as if the work centered her, offered a neutral focus for her mind.

"You may be in no hurry, but you are no doubt bored to tears." She reached for the silver trays stacked on top of the fridge.

He drank the coffee she offered while she lined the trays with green trees and red snowmen, white Christmas balls and multicolored Santas. He even managed to snitch one more while she had her back turned.

The still warm, buttery pastry and sweet sugar glaze melted on his tongue, and when his stomach voiced its undying gratitude, she cast him a cute smile over her shoulder as she left the room, saying, "Be right back."

He really needed to grab a bite to eat. Coffee and cookies wouldn't hold him through his shift at the clinic. Or keep his mind focused and off Brooke Bailey's mouth, which within the last hour or so had become a fixation.

He wanted to kiss her. Tenderly in comfort. Roughly in want. But he wouldn't. Because of JJ. And because, JJ or no, Duncan would want more than a kiss.

He would want the slow burn of her emotions, the fiery sparks of her passion. Any woman with Brooke's sense of life offered a challenge a man would be a fool to turn down.

JJ had a hell of a challenge on his hands, and for the first time a shred of doubt tore through Duncan's faith in his friend. Not about whether or not JJ was worthy, but whether or not Brooke was what he needed. She didn't seem to have the aggressive nature to put up with the demands of JJ's ambitions.

Brooke seemed softer. Driven, yes. But not as competitive as Sally. Definitely not as consumed as JJ. Or as Duncan himself.

She was exactly the woman he wanted.

Damn. That wasn't true. He didn't want anything. He'd made that decision long ago, when work had become his life and doing for others his goal.

Both took up enough of his time that he had very little for himself, which was the point he'd been trying to get to since third grade. To reach a state where every minute of his life was scheduled, leaving him zero time to think. To feel.

No time to wonder what it would be like to have Brooke Bailey beneath him.

"I'm ready."

His gaze snapped to hers. "What?"

"The cookies." She extended two trays. "If you'll take these, I'll get the other two."

He did as she asked and followed her out of the apartment. Once out in the hall, he hooked the toe of one deck shoe behind the front door and gave it a quick jerk shut.

Halfway down the flight of stairs, after too many steps of watching the movements of black and red curves and, heaven help him, reindeer slippers descending in front of him, female chatter reached his ears.

One of the voices belonged to Nettie. But the other...

"Sounds like Lydia's early," Brooke said, making the turn from the landing to the final short flight of steps. "Good thing I baked an extra batch. Between your sticky fingers and Lydia's sweet tooth, these cookies aren't gonna last the night."

Duncan frowned down at the trays he held in both hands. "Guess one more's out of the question?"

"Yes, if you want to live through the night," she said, and laughed.

He followed her from the last step into the lobby, where Nettie and a stately older woman stood posture perfect, hands together, between the Christmas tree and the alcove entry where the stockings hung on the wall.

At the squeak of his deck shoe soles on the floor, Nettie turned. The lines around her mouth deepened when she smiled, adding character to a face etched with dozens of stories. The woman was a work of art. And knew it.

"Oh my, Brooke," Nettie said, moving forward with the small hurried steps that took her everywhere. "I had no idea you were so clever. This house has not seen the touch of such festivity since my dear Walter passed on."

Brooke smiled, a gentle lifting of the corners of her mouth. Duncan felt it. Again.

"So you're pleased?" she asked.

"Pleased?" The older woman's eyes flashed with

merriment. "Dear heart, you are such a blessing. I'm so sorry we haven't thought to do this before. Of course, I realize this time of year usually takes you home."

Duncan watched the subtle play of emotion over Brooke's face. She'd told him why she wasn't going home. But she hadn't told him what it made her feel. Just as well.

He did better setting bones and stitching gashes in the clinic than he did making sense out of feelings.

"No reason to go home this year, Nettie. I'd have that big empty house to myself."

"Well, as much as I know you will miss your folks, as I do my dear Walter," Nettie said, solicitously patting Brooke's hand, "I know our little family will enjoy having you here to spread the bounty of Christmas."

Brooke glanced at Duncan and actually smirked. "I'm not sure everyone is as thrilled about the cheer as you are, Nettie."

A frown creased Nettie's forehead, her brows drawing together. She glared at Duncan, forcefully narrowed one gray eye, then the other, pursed her lips into a full pout. He had to bite back a laugh.

"I assume you are talking about our resident Dr. Grinch," Nettie said to Brooke while shaking a finger in Duncan's direction. "You can be sure, young man, that the next time I have a vacancy I will ask how the applicant feels about Christmas."

Duncan waited for Nettie to put away her scolding finger. Then he stepped in and spoke close to her ear. Lavender tickled his nose. "Good thing for you I made it in under the wire."

"Don't you be sweet-talking me, Duncan Cox. You save that for any young lady who might have something to do with you." She stretched her five feet two inches as high as she could to look him in the eye. "In four years, that charmer J. J. Mackey never gave me half the grief about writing my arthritis prescription that you've given me this past month."

"But you've been feeling better since you've been coming to the clinic to see me, haven't you?" When she put on her poor-wounded-soul face, Duncan laughed. "Don't try that with me, Nettie May. You just hated coming in for the tests I wanted."

"I'm eighty. I deserve a test exemption. A senior citizen special."

"You deserve exactly what you're getting. Quality health care."

"From a cheeky young doctor who needs to learn that the best medicine for an old woman is to get her own way." She delivered a pat to the side of his face.

He caught Brooke's interest in the exchange from the corner of one eye and shrugged. She could think what she wanted. Women usually did. He was the only one who needed to know his dealings with Nettie were purely doctor to patient.

What might appear to involve personal feelings didn't. This was just the way he worked. And as long as he got the results he needed, as long as Nettie remained in good health, he'd continue to treat her the same.

"What do you want us to do with these trays?" he finally asked.

"Brooke knows where they go. Oh. Oh. But first..." Nettie gestured frantically for Brooke to set her trays on the seat of the deacon's bench. Then, taking her arm, she hurried her across the room to the alcove and the stockings on the wall. "You must come here, my dear. I was showing your stockings to Lydia and it appears Santa has made an early visit."

"You're kidding," Brooke said, allowing the ladies to propel her forward, one on each side.

"No, no, no," Lydia said. "Not kidding at all. Not at all. Come see. Come see."

Uh-oh, Duncan thought, watching the slow smile spread over Brooke's face. He shouldn't have been the one to witness her discovery. It should've been JJ's privilege to see those eyes turn so blue.

But, heaven help him, he couldn't look away.

He set the trays he was still holding next to Brooke's, then stepped closer to the tree for a better look. JJ would want to know what happened. Duncan needed to watch for his friend more than he needed to watch for himself.

"I can't believe this," Brooke was saying. "I just hung these this morning." She brushed her fingertips over the cuff of the stocking.

Her nails were short, with pale polish; the bluish tint of veins was evident beneath the light skin of her hand. Her touch was at first hesitant, then sure. As if the feel of the stocking gave her as much pleasure as the anticipation of what she'd find.

Finally, she reached inside and pulled the pear free of the stocking cuff.

And then she smiled. A picture of elation that squeezed hard at the heart he'd always thought too hardened to give, too atrophied to feel. He'd been wrong.

She turned the lacy fruit side to side, examined it from top to bottom, touched a fingertip to the plumes of the bird. Then she looked up, to Lydia, to Nettie. And then to him. Last. To him.

She held the fruit in the palm of her hand like an offering. "Look," she finally said, her voice a blend of childish wonder and womanly awe. "A partridge in a pear tree. On the first day of Christmas."

Ah, hell. Duncan scrubbed a hand over his face as his gut clenched and clenched harder.

JJ didn't have a clue what he was up against. He only knew Brooke on the surface; he'd seen what she had to offer without stopping to consider who she was.

Good thing the problem was JJ's and not Duncan's.

Brooke briefly closed her eyes, opened them and smiled until her face shone brighter than the tree.

When Duncan remembered to breathe, he swore. Because he was the one with the problem, after all.

5

"BROOKE, HON. Be serious," Sally said, straightening the hem of her thigh-length sweater as she crossed from Brooke's kitchen to her living room. "Why would *I* put a partridge in a pear tree in your stocking?"

Brooke glared at her colorful friend. No one should be so blond and so clever and look so good with primary colors splashed in bold geometric shapes around her disgustingly slim hips. "It just seems like a Sally thing to do, that's why."

"It could have been anyone in the building," Sally patiently explained, still not quite happy with the lay of her hem. "Yesterday was Saturday. People were in and out all day long. If they didn't know it before, they now know how much you love the holiday.

"Take it as the gesture of appreciation I'm sure it is." She looked back up then, frowned and shook a motherly finger in Brooke's direction. "And wipe that scowl off your face while you're at it."

Brooke folded her legs beneath her and settled back into the puffy black pillow of a chair sprawled across the biggest part of the living room. She sank down deep and pouted. "It's not fair. I mean, I love surprises. It's the anonymity I hate."

Sally shoved her fingers through her curls and did

her best to growl. It wasn't much more than a tame purr. Brooke laughed. And this time it was Sally who glared. "If I end up bald, it's your fault, you know."

Brooke shook her head. "Those are your hands in your hair, girlfriend."

"I was making a figurative point." Sally lowered her hands and shook the curls back into perfect place. "You have everything ready for tonight?"

"Yes. But don't try to change the subject."

"I thought the reception was the subject. Isn't that why you called me? To go over the last-minute details?"

True, Brooke had. But she'd also wanted to ask Sally about the gift. To look into her big brown eyes while she answered. To make sure her friend wasn't hiding the truth when she said she didn't know who the gift was from.

Brooke couldn't stand not knowing. Surprises weren't a part of her ritual. She'd always been the one to fill the stockings at home, adding the same fruits, nuts and candies to her own as she did to those of the other adults.

Even on Christmas morning, she had a good idea what she'd find in the boxes bearing her name. The majority of the Baileys had an incredible lack of imagination. Brooke usually ended up with more gold-wrapped boxes of chocolates than Lady Godiva had hair.

"Okay." She raised her hands in surrender. "If you swear to me it wasn't you, I'll shut up about it."

Sally got a mischievous sparkle in her eyes. "Brooke,

hon. It's Christmas. I don't have to swear to anything at all."

Brooke growled, and there wasn't anything tame about the sound. "Oh, fine. Just don't expect anything in your stocking but a lump of coal."

"Great." Hands on her hips, Sally cocked her head to the side and slyly smiled. "I needed something to help heat the apartment."

"YOU WERE ACTUALLY THERE when she found the pear?" JJ asked between deep, measured breaths, his steps a thud-thud against the Memorial Park jogging trail.

"Yep," Duncan grunted in return, thinking Houston winters beat the pants off the southern city's unbearable summers. When June rolled around, he'd be longing for the blue skies and cool Seattle days.

JJ turned his head toward Duncan. "What did she say?"

"Not much." By June he'd have to move the exercise routine indoors. The club a few blocks from the apartment had a great indoor track. And a pool.

"She was surprised?"

"Yeah. Real surprised." He wasn't big on weights. Laps around the track and in the pool usually did the trick. He needed to work off tension more than build bulk.

"Did she wonder who it was from?"

"She didn't say." Of course, he could always use a good ab workout. Nothing worse than a lazy gut on a thirty-five-year-old. Especially a doctor who preached nutrition and fitness to his patients. He needed—

JJ grabbed Duncan's arm and jerked him to a stop.

Duncan freed his arm. "What the hell?"

"Look, Dr. Grinch. I'm trying to get a straight answer here." Hands at his waist, JJ inhaled, exhaled to steady his breathing. "What did Brooke say when she found the pear? If you can remember."

Oh, Duncan remembered all right. Doubted he'd forget. Ever. Not so much the words she'd spoken, but the way she'd looked when she'd said them.

The shine of excitement in her eyes. The caress of her fingertips first over the stocking, then over the lace-wrapped pear. The way her lips had parted on a sudden breath, then eased into a smile that lived in his dreams and his days.

"Well?" JJ persisted.

Duncan braced his hands on his knees and hung his head. "I'm thinking."

Thinking about Brooke. Which he didn't want to do. Thinking about the weather was safe. Thinking about exercise was smart. But thinking about Brooke was trespassing and voyeuristic.

A betrayal of JJ's friendship. A betrayal of Duncan's own ideals. His deeply held beliefs. His third-grade vow to never feel.

Brooke made him feel. Even more than she made him think. He didn't want to do either. Damn it to hell.

He straightened. "She said, 'A partridge in a pear tree. On the first day of Christmas.'"

JJ frowned, digested the information. "That's it?"

"Yes," Duncan lied, turning and heading back in the direction they'd come. No way was he about to reveal anything more. Telling JJ of the wonder in her voice, the awe in her expression, would expose too much. Reveal how he felt. About her.

Even though he had no feelings. For her.

"SPEAKING OF HEATING UP," Brooke said. "How did things go with JJ last night?"

Sally flopped down on her stomach into the pile of green-and-grape-colored pillows covering the futon frame that served as Brooke's sofa. She wiggled around until she got comfortable, and braced her chin in one palm. "He's great. Exactly as you said."

"Yeah. So? Details. The board dinner was...?"

"Typically political."

Two words and Sally stopped. So Brooke prodded. "And JJ was...?"

"A smashing success."

Three words this time. This was going to be a long afternoon. "And you were as well, no doubt. Charming the socks off everyone who could be of great help to you barefoot."

Sally looked up at Brooke as if she'd lost her mind. "That was terrible."

Finally. "No more terrible than the lack of information I'm getting here."

Frowning, Sally plucked at a loose thread on the corner of one grape pillow cover. A totally atypical show of nerves.

Uh-oh. "Sal?"

"It was JJ's night. Not mine. You knew that."

"Yes, I knew that. But surely you made a few contacts."

"I met a lot of people, yes."

Nope. This wasn't like Sally at all. "Met. Hmm. And talked, I hope."

"Of course."

The proverbial pulling of teeth. "About your ideas for Mercy's strategy?"

"Not really."

Brooke flopped back in her pillow chair, dumbfounded. "Sally White. A golden career opportunity and you let it get away. I don't know what to say."

"I was busy selling JJ. Not White Publicity."

As quickly as she'd flopped back, Brooke sat forward. "Sally, you're always selling White Publicity. Morning, noon and night."

"I'll sell White Publicity at my meeting with Dr. Howard this week. Last night I was...distracted."

Distracted? Sally? Brooke frowned, then the light dawned and an enormous grin lifted the corners of her mouth. It had worked. Her scheming and maneuvering and near hand-holding had worked. "JJ."

Sally sighed. "JJ."

"I *knew* you two would be perfect for each other." Brooke rubbed greedy hands together. "Tell me everything. Significant. Insignificant. I want it all."

And Sally proceeded to give it to her. Every last detail.

"HOW'D THE BOARD DINNER go?" Duncan asked, taking the bottle of water JJ handed him from the fridge.

JJ widened his eyes in apparent amazement. "Oh, man. You should've been there."

"Had 'em in the palm of your hand, you say."

"And how." JJ slammed the fridge. "Sally was something. Knew just where to steer the conversation without anyone realizing what she'd done. They never knew what hit 'em."

Interesting. Duncan swallowed, backhanded the moisture from his mouth. "Brooke was right then. About Sally knowing her stuff."

"Oh yeah." JJ leaned back against his kitchen counter. "Her agency is after the Mercy account."

Doubly interesting. "Then the dinner was to her advantage as well."

JJ shook his head, lowered the bottle from his mouth. "That's what's so funny. She didn't talk about her business at all. She concentrated on selling me."

Interesting didn't even begin to cover it. "Maybe she's not the shark you thought."

"She's not. But she is. It's hard to explain."

"You don't have to," Duncan said, but JJ went on.

"She's more subtle. Instead of going for the jugular, she sorta just slipped in when no one was looking," he said, making a sliding motion with one hand.

"You gonna see her again?"

"Professionally? After last night I don't think I'll need to."

Duncan took a deep breath and a chance. "Personally, then."

"Nah. My heart belongs to Brooke," JJ said, as casually as he'd said anything tonight. But even as he did, he looked away, as if he didn't want Duncan to catch the flash of uncertainty in his expression.

Duncan had. And he felt...nothing. He felt nothing beyond the pull of his third grade vow.

"Speaking of my heart, today's the second day of Christmas. I need to come up with another gift." He looked at Duncan. "Any ideas for two turtle doves?" He wiggled both brows. "Buddy?"

Ten more days. Duncan could make it ten more days. Then his promise to JJ would be fulfilled and he wouldn't have to think of Brooke except in passing.

"I picked up something last night at that gift shop down the street from the clinic."

"Yeah? Hey, man. I owe ya," JJ said, and playfully punched Duncan in the arm.

"Just keep your love life to yourself from now on and we'll call it even."

"You gonna tell me what it is?"

"C'mon." Duncan motioned for him to follow. "I'll show you."

"Great. I can drop it in her stocking before the reception." He headed toward the door, cast a glance to his friend. "You are coming tonight, right?"

"Yeah," Duncan said, avoiding his friend's searching gaze. Now if he could figure out how to avoid Brooke as easily, he might actually survive this evening.

Enjoying it was, of course, out of the question.

BY THE TIME Brooke stepped into the lobby, the reception was in full swing. Nettie had shooed her upstairs earlier, telling her that after all the work she'd done yesterday and the time she'd devoted to last-minute details today she deserved a rest.

Brooke had rested a bit. She'd showered. She'd done her hair and makeup. She'd changed clothes seven times, finally settling on a pair of forest green flats, matching lace tights and a formfitting red knit dress with a short, flippy skirt. The Christmas colors suited her mood, the style suited her body.

She caught her reflection in one of the lobby's scrolled and gilded mirrors as she walked past. Though she wasn't happy with her lack of fortitude to stick with the first outfit she'd chosen, the dress *did* give her complexion a bit of color...as if that actually mattered!

Nettie was acting as hostess. Brooke didn't need to dress the part. All she needed was to look as deliciously festive as possible in order to bring a bit of Christmas cheer to Duncan Cox's face. There. She'd said it. She was using her womanly wiles toward an ulterior end.

The Grinch would learn how to smile.

And before she was finished, he would learn to appreciate the spirit of Christmas. The season provided immeasurable joy. She wanted him to open his eyes and see that for himself. He might never embrace all that the holiday offered, but he couldn't be human and ignore the obvious.

The lobby of the apartment building was full. All of the residents mingling, several with dates. Head held high, Lydia drifted through the small room, moving from group to group, a tray of snacks in her hand, her caftan flowing, as if her regal bearing made this more than an informal get-together.

Nettie hovered near the table of drinks, replenishing cups of wassail, spiking more than one with her home-made apple wine. She spied Brooke, greeting her with a broad smile and a hand lifted in welcome. A smile lined with age, a hand bent to the will of the years.

At the familiarity of the gesture, a pang of sorrow struck Brooke hard. Nettie brought so many memories of Nanna to mind. But dwelling on the past, especially at this time of year, was nothing if not unproductive.

Brooke knew it, knew the best thing for her to do was to remember the joy of times spent with her grand-mother and draw on the pleasure found in thoughts of Christmases past. To let the thoughts and memories feed on one another until this year was behind her.

She made her way around the periphery of the room, needing that little bit of time to pull herself to-gether. This was going to be a great Christmas. There wasn't a doubt in her mind, or in her heart.

"Brooke, dear," Nettie said, taking both of Brooke's hands in hers. "We must do this again next year. I so enjoy the company of these young people. My, what opinions. What enthusiasm." Nettie fluttered her lashes. "What romance."

Brooke freed her hands, wrapped her arms around the small woman and hugged. Poignant tears pricked her eyes and she blinked to keep them from spilling. "Of course we'll do it next year," she said at Nettie's ear.

She made the promise to herself. It was a promise

she would keep. This year the distraction provided her salvation. Next year another tenant might reap the benefit.

"I hope you don't mind," she heard Nettie say.

Brooke straightened and looked around. "Mind?"

"That I hung the mistletoe."

Uh-oh. She glanced in the direction Nettie indicated, where hanging from the arch of the alcove opening she spied the familiar ribbon-wrapped bundle of green leaves and white berries.

"Of course I don't mind," she assured Nettie. "But that mistletoe is the oldest trick in the book, you know. Your matchmaking efforts are getting out of hand."

Nettie's glee was the stuff that tugged at the heart-strings. She clapped her hands together. "Don't be denying an old woman her fun now, Brooke Bailey. Lydia and I have bets on who's going to get the first kiss." Nettie frowned and pursed her lips in aggravation. "It is definitely not supposed to be one of us."

Brooke turned in time to see Lydia gliding closer to Pat, the engineer who lived on the fourth floor. Each step in reverse put Pat that much nearer the alcove arch and the mistletoe. But he'd met his match in the distinguished dowager. She was intent on having her way.

Brooke crossed her arms, raised a brow and spoke from the side of her mouth to Nettie. "You going to do anything about that?"

"I just don't know." Nettie tapped an index finger to her chin. "Do you think she'll hurt him?"

It wasn't Pat Brooke was worried about. "Only if she

doesn't stop and backs him into the Christmas tree. If that happens I'll hurt both of them."

"Until then I suppose we should let nature take its course. It would be a shame to deny an old woman her fun," Nettie said, just as Lydia made the final move that put Pat under the mistletoe.

She hooked a gaunt elbow around the engineer's neck and smacked him up close and personal. The room erupted in cheers and laughter. Brooke joined in. The astonishment on Pat's face was worth the admission to any feature film.

Just then a flash of white from a crisp oxford-cloth shirt caught her eye and she looked up to see Duncan Cox. He stood in the corner of the alcove talking to JJ and Terri, the accountant who lived in the apartment between Sally and Brooke.

The Grinch of Mercy Hospital. She could see it in his face. Grim. Sour. As if the mood in the room gave him indigestion.

He was ready to bolt. And she wasn't about to let him. If for no other reason than she intended to prove to both of them that Christmas had the power she'd attributed to it her entire life.

He met her eyes, his gaze lifting suddenly from Terri's face to Brooke's as if he'd heard her thoughts and demanded equal time. She lifted the cup of wassail Nettie had handed her in a sort of toast, an acceptance of the challenge she saw in his eyes. He did the same.

Then, without taking his eyes from her, he excused himself from JJ and Terri and headed toward her.

He had that this-lobby-isn't-big-enough-for-both-of-us look. Brooke wouldn't doubt that he was here against his will. At least the part of his will that required conscious thought. The same part that had so much trouble with Christmas being celebrated right under his nose.

It was his unconscious will she needed to work on. Because there she would find the heart of the Grinch.

"Nice turnout," he said when he reached her.

"Of course," she replied. "I expected nothing less."

"Bringing joy to all those around you." His gaze canvased the room. "I see you've succeeded."

"Not quite," she answered, setting her cup on the table behind her, then wishing she hadn't because she wasn't quite sure what to do with her hands.

She finally clasped her fingers at the small of her back and leaned against the wall. Duncan moved in closer at the same time Nettie tiptoed away.

The buzz of talk faded into the background. Brooke heard only the rapid beat of her heart, felt nothing but her skin raise in gooseflesh. Duncan braced a hand on the wall near her head.

The sleeves of his white shirt were cuffed, tempting her to slip her fingers underneath. His skin was golden, the hair a shade darker—the result a temptation she found hard to resist.

"If you're trying to bring that joy to me, you won't succeed. I told you I don't celebrate Christmas."

"I know."

"The fact that I'm here doesn't change that."

"I know."

"I'm only here because of Nettie. And JJ."

"I know."

"Is there anything you don't know?" His coffee-cocoa eyes darkened.

Good. She'd gotten a reaction. It was a beginning. "One thing, yes."

"And that is?"

"Why you feel the need to explain yourself to me."

"No big deal. I just didn't want you to get the wrong idea about me being here," he said, and brought his beer bottle to his lips.

She watched his throat work as he swallowed, then quickly looked away. Thoughts entertained in private were one thing. But standing this close and thinking those same thoughts, wondering about the texture of his neck exposed above his shirt collar, imagining the up-close smell of clean warmth, thinking of the taste of resilient skin, was something else.

A shudder of near arousal stole through her, tightening her breasts as well as her thighs. She crossed her arms and searched for a safe distraction. Sally stood talking to JJ and she caught her eye.

Brooke inclined her head in a silent question intended to indicate interest in the progression of *things* with JJ. Sally did the same in return, looking from Brooke to Duncan. Brooke widened her eyes, vehemently shook her head. Sally arched a brow in disbelief.

A chuckle tickled its way up Brooke's throat.

"What's so funny?" Duncan asked.

Brooke waved a hand. "Just Sally and...just boring girl stuff."

The corner of Duncan's mouth quirked. "Yeah. Right. Boring."

Ah, almost a smile. She narrowed a threatening eye. "I'd tell ya, but then I'd have to kill ya."

He did smile at that. A true smile of the sort she had never seen on his face. As if he'd let his guard down enough to find the humor in the situation. The smile was brilliant and it stunned her, tugging at feelings she hadn't felt for a long while.

So the Grinch had a heart after all. The discovery pleased her in ways that it probably shouldn't have.

She had no business allowing him to please her. Still, his grin was contagious and hers grew wider in direct proportion. "I knew you would enjoy yourself."

"I never said I couldn't enjoy myself."

"Ah, that's right. Just that you don't like Christmas."

"Exactly."

"I have time to change your mind. It's only the second day of Christmas."

If she hadn't been looking into his face, closely watching the way the Christmas tree lights shone in his eyes, she would've missed that quick flash that triggered her female intuition.

Surely he didn't know anything about the partridge in a pear tree. Unless it was from JJ instead of from Sally. Or Nettie. Or Lydia. Or Terri. Or any of the others she'd run through.

No. It wasn't JJ. It was a frivolous gift and not his style.

"You know," Duncan said, breaking into her

thoughts, "your early visit from Santa was the talk of the room before you got here."

"You're kidding. I wonder how..." She grimaced. "Sally."

He shrugged. "She may have started the talk. But it didn't take long to get around. Or for everyone to start wondering when you'd get here."

"Why?"

"To see your reaction when you checked your stocking tonight."

She looked at him, over his shoulder, back at his face. His eyes never left hers. Oh, no. Not here. Not now. Not in front of all these people.

She'd sensed the stares earlier and attributed them to the normal acknowledgment of a hostess by her guests. But now the looks took on a peculiar distinction and she saw the curiosity she'd missed before.

The discovery of the first gift had been semiprivate, witnessed only by Nettie, Lydia and Duncan. Brooke had been able to hide what exactly the partridge in a pear tree made her feel. About home. About Christmas. About receiving a gift that came with thought rather than a prewrapped box of chocolates.

The giver knew of her love for Christmas and had given accordingly. Her money was on Sally, who knew of Brooke's love, knew as well the reason she'd been devastated at the prospect of not going home, of spending her holiday with friends rather than family.

Yes, it made perfect sense. Sally was involving as many people as possible in Brooke's Christmas. And Brooke couldn't have asked for a better friend.

"Well?" Duncan prompted. "Are you going to stand in the corner all night or show us more of that Christmas spirit you're always harping on?"

"Harping on?" He didn't understand. He had no reason to. Which was fine. This moment would be publicly shared, but privately savored. The gift, the gesture behind it, as well as the dawning realization that these people—friends, not family—were waiting for her reaction to the discovery...oh, yes. She would savor each.

"Don't watch," she said, then stood on tiptoe, placed her hand on his shoulder and whispered into his ear. "This might make you like Christmas."

Then she ducked under his raised arm and walked into the alcove, ignoring the slamming of her heart against her ribs, the suggestion of his muscled shoulder beneath her palm, the tickle of his hair against her lips and the very real, very pronounced doubt she saw in his eyes.

Yes. The moment was one he needed to witness as much as one she needed to experience. But then the spirit of Christmas worked in mysterious ways.

Even on the heart of a Grinch.

6

DUNCAN REALLY DIDN'T WANT to see this again. Not here. Not now. Not in front of all these people.

He damned his grand twelve-days-of-Christmas scheme. Damned JJ for getting him into this mess. Damned himself most of all.

Somewhere along the way Duncan should've learned to say no to the one person who'd been there for him since third grade, the only person who'd been there for him his entire life. But he didn't have it in him to refuse his best friend.

So he prayed for the thunder and lightning that threatened outside with the fury of a true Texas winter to deliver on their stormy promise and plunge the room into darkness. Not that it would do a bit of good.

The light in Brooke's eyes was too bright.

He shouldn't have noticed, but since he had he should've promptly forgotten. He couldn't. And he didn't. Because as much as he dreaded the prospect of witnessing her discovery, he needed a rational explanation for the rapid beating of his heart.

He blamed it on her eyes.

She was a gorgeous woman. That black hair pulled back and wrapped up in a green hair-tie thing. That sexy red dress that hinted and teased in the classiest way possible. That inviting smile. And those big blue eyes.

Any man who got a close look at the entire package and didn't come away with a tight chest was dead. Or lying. Duncan was neither.

So he blamed it on her eyes.

But rational or not, the attraction of her eyes barely touched the iceberg tip of the reasons he couldn't breathe. There was more here than the obvious physical attraction.

He had no intention of slicing and dicing and analyzing what it was, though he would make the admission that the *what* ran deep. Mercy had a staff of psychologists already itching to get their couches under him.

He was saved from further irritating musings by the round of applause that went up in the room. It was time for the show. He stood with his back to the Christmas tree, behind the rest of the small but boisterous crowd, and watched Brooke.

Her mouth was moving, saying words he couldn't hear from so far away, or above the roaring in his head. Her motions were economical but fluid and elegant. Her hands skimmed her collar, then the cuff of the stocking. She reached inside to remove the gift.

He shifted where he stood, shaking off the beginnings of hard arousal, shoving his fists in the pockets of his slacks to have something to do with his hands. He wanted another drink. He wanted to run.

He wanted to touch her. More than anything, he wanted to touch her.

Most of all, though, he watched her eyes. The way her long lashes dipped, the way she looked up from beneath them. The way laughter brought moisture and the moisture glistened and the glistening brightened the blue until it blazed.

He started to look away, but she caught him with her gaze. Caught him and held him, and he couldn't move. He couldn't move. The breath he inhaled burned. The muscles he held stiff started to ache. He started to ache. His fists clenched. His chest tightened. His lower body stirred, hardened.

The buzz of his pager saved his pride—if not his life.

BROOKE GENTLY CARESSED the delicate lines of the ceramic sculpture she held in one palm. The two tiny doves perched on the replica of a low bush perfectly represented the second day of Christmas. The birds were exquisite in detail, contrasting with the abstract lines starkly resembling bare branches.

Others around her admired the workmanship while she silently absorbed the particulars in a heartbeat. The same length of time it took Duncan to leave.

His departure came as no surprise. His stance had grown more stiff and withdrawn the closer she got to the discovery of the gift. As if he had a stake in it. Which was ridiculous.

The front door latched behind him. No doubt he'd deny his exit was a retreat, but such a denial carried no weight. Not tonight. He'd been wanting to go since their eyes first met after she'd walked into the room. Possibly even before.

Quite honestly, she'd wondered if he would come. Not that his presence should have mattered, but it did. She wanted to include him in the holiday celebration, to show him the joy.

And that was why he'd left. She'd seen him check his pager and would never accuse him of staging his means of escape. He might run, but he would do so honorably.

No, he'd left because she had accomplished the night's mission. She'd shown him the joy; she'd seen the light dawn in his eyes. The second day of Christmas and she was close to making him see the true meaning of the holiday.

By the morning of the twenty-fifth, he'd be a convert. And she would be...what?

Alone? She lived alone. It wasn't the same as being lonely, and shouldn't matter. She had friends, dear friends. Friends she deemed closer than family. Closer than family...

She blew out a breath as the realization became a deeply emotional awareness. Yes, of course, she missed Nanna. Desperately and without question.

But even as she acknowledged the thought, came the understanding, the near painful awakening that she had no other reason to go home. There wasn't another family member with whom she wished to spend this Christmas.

Oh, God.

What did that say about her commitment to family, the value she'd always placed on the same? What did it say about the Christmases she'd orchestrated for the Baileys over the past fifteen years?

And what did it say about her lifelong insistence that family meant home, that home meant belonging?

Oh, God. Oh, God.

She looked up through misty eyes to see Sally standing in the alcove archway, motioning her forward. Brooke excused herself from Terri and Pat and was halfway to Sally's side when she felt a hand on her arm.

Nettie's arthritic grip was firm, her gray eyes solemn. "He'll be back. I'm sure it was the hospital that called."

"Are you talking about Duncan?" Brooke asked, summoning the disinterest she knew she should feel. Or at least the disinterest she knew she should show Nettie. "I thought I saw him slip out earlier."

"Slip, ha. Skulk is more like it." Nettie patted at her coiffed hair, frowned when she found a curl out of place, tucked it back. Then, hand still on the back of her head, she lifted a sly eye Brooke's way. "I saw the two of you cozying up in the corner."

"Cozying up?" Brooke made sure her tone was accusing, even though she was certain Nettie would see through the accusation. "You mean that corner where we stood talking once *you* skulked away?"

Eighty years of practiced innocence. Nettie had the expression mastered. "Did I do that?"

"Yes, you did and you know it," Brooke scolded. "Now, let me see what Sally has on her mind before I finally strangle you once and for all."

Nettie tittered like only an eighty-year-old match-maker could. "Why, if I left the romance up to you young folks, there wouldn't be a speck of tomfoolery taking place under my roof. What with my dear Walter having passed at such a young and virile time in life."

Brooke gave Nettie a quick hug. "I think if you let nature take its course all us young folks will do just fine."

"Well, go on with you then. Your friend is waiting. And Brooke, my dear," Nettie added before Brooke got away. "You might want to mention to Sally what exactly she's standing under and who she's standing there with."

Brooke's head snapped around. She looked up at the mistletoe, down to Sally's face, over to JJ, then back. Sally frowned, then mimicked Brooke's motions. Both women's eyes widened at the same time, both mouths formed astonished O's. Then one settled into a smile of satisfaction, one into panic.

What a perfect setup, Brooke thought as others in the room became aware of the kiss waiting to happen. There was no way Sally could blame Brooke for what surely was about to take place. This was Nettie's matchmaking, pure and simple, and in this case a gem of an idea at work.

Brooke was going to kill JJ if he didn't follow through. But as he was talking over Sally's shoulder to Lydia, a gentle prompting was definitely in order.

Brooke walked forward, fixing her friend with a stern look promising severe repercussions should Sally move. Brooke was going to see this kiss through to the end.

"Sorry," she said once she reached Sally's side. "I got hung up with Nettie."

"That's okay. I just wanted to see the figurine." Sally's voice carried a rare touch of nervousness.

Brooke took full advantage of the opening. "As if you haven't already?"

"When would I have seen it?"

Ah, two could play this game. "Maybe when you bought it? When you put it in my stocking?"

"C'mon, Brooke. Why would I put two turtle doves in your stocking?"

"Oh, I don't know." Brooke crossed her arms. "Just seems like something you'd do."

"I give up," Sally said with a toss of her hands. "Believe what you will."

"I always do," Brooke answered, and turned to JJ despite Sally's visual protest. "Uh, JJ?"

He looked around at the sound of her voice, flashed his dimples. "Miss Merry Christmas. Having a good time? Enjoying Santa's early visits?"

"I can honestly answer yes to both."

"Good." JJ stepped closer to the two women. He nodded toward the figurine Brooke held. "Looks like the second day of Christmas. Guess this has been a good evening for you."

"You're right. It has." The time had come. "But I don't think it's as good as yours is about to be." She cast both eyes upward, making certain to take a step in reverse so he could see who it was standing beside him under the mistletoe.

He did see, and the expression on his face as he looked at Sally pleased Brooke in ways she'd never thought possible. It was a look of surprise, yes, and a sporting one at that, like he would go along with the fun in order to keep Sally from embarrassment if nothing else.

But there was more to his look, a hint of an emotion Brooke knew to be directed solely at Sally.

An emotion he'd never directed at Brooke.

She knew then, at that very moment, that her instincts had been right. She was glad to be able to call JJ a friend. Glad to have settled once and for all that they could never be more.

And especially glad for the unexpected matchmaking thought that had drifted in on the cosmos and dropped into her lap. She had a feeling the entire room was about to witness an exceptional moment.

JJ rubbed his palms together, to the delight of the female onlookers and accompanying wolf whistles from the males. Sally crossed her arms, lifted her chin and cocked one hip to the side as if to say, "Give it your best shot, big boy."

Slowly, JJ stepped closer. Defiantly, Sally resisted, her shoulders canted back. He placed his hands there, pulled her forward, sent his palms skimming up her neck. He grazed her jawline with his thumbs and Sally's eyelids fluttered, drifted closed.

When he speared his fingers into her hair, her lips parted. When he leaned into her upper body, she did the same. And when his lips met hers, settled, sampled, explored, she melted against him, wrapped her arms around his shoulders and whimpered.

Brooke swiped a knuckle under her eye and sighed.

EVEN ONCE THEY'D REACHED her front door, JJ kept his arm around Sally's shoulders. He didn't want to let go. Strange that he couldn't figure out why.

She'd been the hit of last night's board dinner, knocking the collective socks off the other doctors as well as the other doctors' wives. He'd watched her work the crowd and found it hard to keep a disinterested expression in the face of her performance.

Still, what could have been an act for his sake rang one-hundred-percent true. Every word, every reply or question had been right on. Sally knew her stuff. Only one thing bothered him about the whole night.

When he'd mentally put Brooke in Sally's place, the image hadn't meshed. As if the territory belonged to one woman and not the other.

Not that there was a thing he'd want to change about Brooke Bailey. It was just that last night Sally had seemed so in her element. Brooke had seemed more in hers yesterday, doing for Nettie. He wasn't sure he needed Brooke's nurturing as much as he could use Sally's direction. This was a time in his life when every decision he made would affect his future.

And the only decision he wanted to make now was to figure out the best time to kiss Sally again.

He very much wanted to kiss her again.

"Okay."

"I can?"

Sally frowned. "You can what?"

Man, he'd seriously lost it. "Nothing. Okay what?"

She looked at him askance. "Okay, we're here. My place. Remember?"

He wasn't likely to forget. When she put her hand on the doorknob, turned and started to push it open, he covered her wrist with his fingers to stop her.

She looked confused, then wary, but finally released her hold and stepped away from the door. "JJ?"

He shoved one hand through his hair, then parked both fists at his hips. Where did he even start? "About that kiss..."

Brows arched, she crossed her arms over her chest and stood tall. "Yes?"

Now where did he go? "I didn't mean—"

"I know you didn't mean it," Sally said.

It was almost as if she were giving him a way out. He didn't want a way. Wasn't going to take it. This had to be said and said now.

"No. That's just it. I did mean it," he admitted, then hurried on. "But what I wanted to say was that I didn't mean for it to happen that way. That fast. In front of everyone."

"How did you mean it to happen?"

"I didn't mean it to." When she pressed her lips together he felt a reaction deep in his gut and groaned. "I can't say what I'm trying to say."

"Why not? Words are simple enough. Just put one after another. Like you do your feet when walking," she finished, and smiled.

"Funny," he answered, and relaxed. "I shouldn't have kissed you. In public. Like that."

"Like what?" she innocently asked.

With all those hands and lips and teeth and tongues, he wanted to say. Instead he said, "Like we were lovers."

She quieted then, stepped back against the wall beside the door. "You're right."

"I am?" That wasn't what she was supposed to say. He moved closer.

She nodded, looked up into his eyes. "There's only one reason for what happened downstairs."

"Would that reason be Brooke or Nettie?" he asked, placing both palms against the wall on either side of her head.

"Neither."

He got as close as he could, smelled her, her skin, her hair, fresh and sweet and female. "Then what?"

"It must have been the mistletoe."

No. She was wrong. And very slowly, very explicitly, he showed her just how very.

BROOKE SLID ONTO the deacon's bench, dropped the plastic garbage bag at her feet. She let her head fall back, her eyes drift shut. A pillow and a quilt and she'd be in heaven.

"You want me to get that?" Nettie asked.

Brooke looked up. Nettie had one arm wrapped around the Crock-Pot she'd used to heat the wassail. The other hand held two empty cookie trays.

Typical Nettie. Trying to do everything at once.

Brooke smiled. "Unless you plan to carry this bag with your teeth, I'm not sure how you'd get it to the Dumpster."

Nettie frowned. "Good point. Especially since these aren't my teeth."

Eighty years of sassiness. Nettie was a classic. And Brooke wouldn't have had her any other way. "I think that falls under the heading of too much information, my dear."

A titter escaped Nettie's lips. "I'm an old woman. I've earned the right to say whatever I like."

"I suppose you have."

"Nothing to suppose. Being eighty comes with a lot of freedoms, and I intend to take full advantage. Just wait until you get here. You'll see."

Brooke rubbed at the back of her neck. "You think I'll reach eighty?"

"With the right man around to keep you from working yourself to death you'll probably live to be a hundred."

"I see. A man is the answer to my problems?" Not that she had any problems....

"Men seem to come in two types. They're either problems or they're solutions."

Brooke wondered which type Duncan was before realizing that, to her, he was neither. He was nothing but a neighbor and, okay, a friend. "Well, then. I'm probably better off on my own, wouldn't you say? I sure don't need a problem. And I do fairly well finding the solutions I need."

"You found one yet to explain why you're so gung-ho on spreading Christmas cheer? Not that I mind in the least," Nettie continued when Brooke would have interrupted. "I was just curious as to when you would figure it all out."

"There's nothing to figure out," Brooke answered. She missed Nanna—especially now, dealing with her first Christmas lacking that one vital element she'd always counted on at this time of year.

She didn't need to delve deeper. She didn't. Truly. Not when tonight she'd already questioned her feelings for home and family.

Nettie smiled a gentle smile. "There's always something to figure out. I'm eighty. I know. Tonight I figured out that mistletoe hung in just the right spot can work miracles."

"It was a kiss. Not a miracle," Brooke said, though she thought much the same thing.

"Dear, you do have some figuring out to do if you don't know that a kiss *is* a miracle."

And leaving Brooke with that bit of profound wisdom, Nettie slowly turned and made her way to her first-floor apartment.

Brooke watched her landlady go, thinking that the wisdom of years was a precious gift, the giver generous, the recipient blessed. She wondered if and when she reached Nettie's age, who she'd pass her wisdom to.

It certainly wouldn't be a family of her own. Not at the rate she was going. Probably a good thing. Since she was coming to wonder if what she believed about family held half the truths she'd once thought. Or if she was only a dreamer, believing in the fantasy and the fairy tales of—

The front door opened and Duncan walked into the lobby, which was empty of everything but Christmas, Brooke and the bag of trash. Exactly the way she would have chosen for him to find her. Reindeer slippers yesterday, garbage today. Good thing she wasn't trying to make a good impression.

He saw her. Before the door had even closed behind him. Nettie had doused the lights when she'd left, but the tiny white electric candles on the Christmas tree offered Brooke light enough to see. To see his eyes. The way they'd flashed before he could pull in the response she knew he hated having let her see.

"Everyone gone already?" he asked, stepping toward her reluctantly, part emergency-room trauma physician, part Grinch.

She saw pieces of both, watched the competent battle the cranky even while she kicked a toe at the garbage bag and strove for humor. "No one here but us trashy types."

That one corner of his mouth quirked upward. He stepped closer. "The last ones to leave a party usually are."

She bit back a dozen smart comments, but offered him a smile. "You see a lot of that type?"

"I see enough. Of all types."

"I'm sure."

Hands shoved deep in his pockets, he made his way slowly forward, finally turning to sit at the other end of the bench. He leaned against the back, stretched out his legs.

She tried not to notice exactly how long they were, or how the expensive fabric of his slacks draped over his runner's legs. She also tried not to notice the weight of his sigh.

"Long night?"

He shook his head. "Just a bad one."

Brooke wasn't sure what to say, didn't know if he'd take a question as prying, if he even wanted to talk. But the silence wasn't uncomfortable.

In fact, she found herself more relaxed than she'd been all evening. She found that she liked the feeling. It seemed to mesh perfectly with this time of year. Even more so with the company of this man.

That meant trouble.

She went ahead and pried. "A bad one?"

He nodded. The motion snagged her peripheral vision.

"Gunshot."

She couldn't stop the way her breath caught, the way her heart suddenly started. "Oh, my. I'm sorry. I shouldn't have asked."

"It's all right."

"It has to be hard. To see that."

"It's not easy. Also not surprising."

"Why not surprising?"

He turned then, shifted on the bench and faced her. "It's the time of year. This father was just fired. Couldn't face disappointing his kids. No money equals no gifts. So he used his hunting rifle to make sure he wouldn't have to see their faces Christmas morning."

Brooke couldn't think over the beat of her heart, couldn't hear beyond the silence of the room, the echo of his words.

"Unfortunately," Duncan continued, "his attempt at suicide failed. Now his kids will never have a normal Christmas again. If they ever have one at all." He closed his eyes, slumped back. His head lolled on his shoulders.

Brooke worried the hem of her skirt, pleating and re-pleating the ruffle to keep her fingers busy, to keep her hands in her lap and off of Duncan's weary neck.

"I can't figure out why they do it," he said, talking to himself more than to her. "It's just a holiday. A god-damn commercial, greedy, twenty-four-hour time frame. It's not worth what it's going to cost this family. Ever. Nothing is worth a child's life."

He hadn't said "father's," he'd said "child's." There had to be a reason. Not a logical one or a rational one. He was beyond both at this point. The reason was not even one related to the tragedy he'd witnessed tonight. It was one so personal and lived with that rational logic couldn't touch it.

"You're right. It's not. But there's more involved here than the holiday."

He looked her way sharply. "Think so? Think losing a job at the Fourth of July would've had the same im-pact? Let's see. How would he have worded *that* note? 'Dear family, I can't afford to buy firecrackers this year so I thought I'd try to blow my head off instead.'"

Duncan leaned forward, braced his elbows on his knees, hung his laced hands between. Dejection settled around him as if it had been hovering, expecting this chance.

She wondered. "Duncan, did you lose a parent? At Christmas? When you were a child?"

He shook his head, his mouth grim. "No. I knew where they were. Every minute."

His knuckles whitened. Even in the dim light Brooke could see his knuckles whiten. Frustration? Futility? Anger? Perhaps a combination. Definitely a reaction he wanted to keep contained.

Definitely one she wanted to explore. This was the heart of his feelings for Christmas. Of that she had no doubt.

"You knew where they were. Does that mean they weren't with you? Did they spend their Christmases elsewhere?" Abandonment could explain a lot. Especially if he'd been left alone at Christmas.

"They were with me. When their schedules permitted. Which wasn't often. It's hard to take a break from playing Santa to the needy masses." He rose wearily to his feet and grabbed the trash bag. "You goin' up?"

She was now. And she wasn't going to tell him that she'd planned to haul the trash outside, not to her apartment. This wasn't the time for interruptions, not when the flow had become so interesting. She could deal with an extra bag of garbage tomorrow.

Stretching her arms overhead, she slowly stood. "Yeah. I need to. It's been a long day. And I have work tomorrow. And, uh, I can manage the garbage."

"It's okay. I don't mind." He motioned for her to go ahead.

She headed for the stairs, his footsteps soft on the floor behind her, and she had to fight the urge to reach up and smooth back her ponytail. Her hair was the least of her worries. Right now she needed to figure out a way to turn the conversation back to Santa Claus in the time it took to climb to the second floor.

The Christmas tree gently illuminated the small alcove, lending just the right amount of light to sparkle off the gold paint on the cuffs of the stockings. Her gaze caught the outline of the small bulge in the last one in the row.

"Wait," she said, and made a quick detour to retrieve the two turtle doves. When she turned back, he was waiting for her, standing in the alcove archway, underneath the mistletoe.

Oh, how she was tempted. Especially after watching that unexpected flare between JJ and Sally earlier tonight. She wondered if Duncan knew about that, about the way JJ felt for Sally.

"Why are you smiling?"

She looked into his eyes. "Did you know you're standing under the mistletoe?"

7

DUNCAN GLANCED UP at the alcove archway, then back in Brooke's direction. A hint of a true smile crossed his mouth. "Just my luck. Stuck under the mistletoe with the trash."

Brooke couldn't help it. She laughed, loudly and fully, and the temptation grew. And grew. But she wouldn't give in. She wouldn't. That didn't mean she wouldn't enjoy the moment. Or take it a bit further to see what else Duncan might reveal.

Learning more about him couldn't hurt in her quest to change his mind about Christmas. Especially now that he'd let slip just enough to truly rouse her curiosity. "You missed it earlier. Quite a show."

"Here?" He gestured overhead. "Lydia catch another unsuspecting victim?"

Brooke stayed where she was, her fingers wrapped around the figurine. "JJ."

His eyes widened, flashed golden in the light. "She caught Jay?"

"Not Lydia," Brooke answered, shaking her head. "Sally."

She watched a dozen thoughts cross his mind, the implications of his friend and her friend and where that kiss might or might not lead.

"Wow," he finally said, set the trash bag at his feet, parked a hand at his waist. The other rubbed at the back of his neck. "That surprises me. About JJ."

"Why?" Her interest peaked. "He was a good sport about it. So was Sally. Better than I think I would've been," she added, immediately regretting the admission when the doubting Thomas look in his eyes told her he planned to change the conversational direction.

He crossed his arms and stayed where he was, under the mistletoe, as if his bold defiance of tradition presented a challenge to her Christmas spirit. "You? Miss Merry Christmas? Not a good sport?"

She wouldn't let his teasing get to her. But she now knew she could get to him by being honest. She stroked the figurine again. "I'm not big on public displays. When it comes to certain things."

"Like kissing?"

She nodded, then took her honesty further. "At least a kiss like that."

One of Duncan's eyebrows went up. "Oh yeah?"

Oh yeah. That kiss had moved her. She couldn't tell him how much or in what ways. Wasn't even ready to make that admission to herself.

The admission that she'd thought of him, Duncan. Had wanted to kiss him, Duncan.

No. She wasn't ready to make that admission at all. "I guess you'd have to ask one of them about 'oh yeah.' What I don't understand, though, is why JJ kissing Sally would surprise you."

Duncan lifted one shoulder in a shrug. "He's always been a one woman kinda guy."

This time she took her honesty to the limit. "So. Why can't Sally be that woman?"

He regarded her then, intently, intimately, looking at her with those hooded bird-of-prey eyes. The dim light gave that look a quality that had Brooke wanting to take a step back almost as much as she wanted to take one forward, to feel that gaze up close, inches away, focused and clear and certain in its purpose.

He glanced down to the floor, then back up, shoved his fists in his pockets and said, "I thought you were that woman."

She knew he'd thought that because JJ had thought that. Perhaps until as recently as tonight. But JJ didn't think that anymore. And Duncan needed to know the truth. She needed him to know the truth.

"JJ and I are good friends," she said. "We've dated. A few times. We both knew that was as far as it was going to go. He needs a go-getter. Like Sally. And I need…"

She let the thought trail off, stroked a finger over the figurine. This was an area she wasn't ready to face, let alone discuss with Duncan Cox.

"You like that?"

At his question, she looked up. He nodded toward the figure. She smiled. "I love it. It's perfect. The best second day of Christmas I could have imagined."

He seemed to think a moment, to consider what had passed, to dwell on her words, as if trying to understand or make sense of the same type of musings that had her tied up in knots. As if waiting to speak until he ordered his thoughts.

She moved to the side of the alcove, closer to where he stood while avoiding where he stood. She wanted, needed to be close when he said what was on his mind. Wanted, needed to see his eyes.

He kept them on the figurine. "That was a public display. Finding that in your stocking."

"It wasn't so bad. You'd prepared me. The crowd was a friendly one," she teasingly said. "And after yesterday's pear, I had an idea it would be something simple that I wouldn't mind sharing."

She balanced the birds in her palm, concentrated on them as well as her thoughts. "There are other things that would be harder in public."

"Like a kiss."

They were back to that. She'd thought talking of that type of intimacy with Duncan would make her uneasy. But strangely it didn't.

She found it wasn't hard at all to raise her eyes to his. "Yes. Like a kiss."

After a long, thoughtful moment, his eyes flared, darkened, grew powerful in their regard. "Or like singing?" he finally asked.

How was she supposed to inhale when he looked at her that way with those eyes? Those coffee-cocoa, dangerously perceptive eyes. "I don't sing in public."

"You sing in private. In the mornings. When you shower," he said, his voice a low, private whisper by the time the last of the words escaped.

"You hear that? Me? Singing?" *Please say no. Please say no.*

But he nodded. And said, "Yes. I hear you singing."

She ignored her stiff shoulders, her tight jaw, the ceramic lines of the tiny figurine cutting into her fingers, and strove for nonchalance. "Isn't that where people are supposed to sing? In the shower?"

"I don't," he answered.

And, after her breath took flight at the end of a long sigh, she managed to say, "I know."

"I wondered about that. If you realized."

Realized what? That they were both wet and naked at virtually the same time each day? How could she be human and female and not realize? She smoothed back her ponytail. "Sure. The pipes are old. I hear them. I hear the floor creak under the tub. Or I guess what I hear is the tub creaking over my ceiling."

When he stepped away from the archway, his toe caught the corner of the trash bag. Bottles clinked and cans clattered on the short slide across the floor. The air in the alcove grew warm and close; the scent of the spruce needles was pungent.

His shoulders were broad, his body fit, and she licked her lips. He drew his hands from his pockets. His steps brought him close and she trembled. The tiny Christmas candles glittered off the lightest strands in his hair, caught sparks of light and heat in his eyes.

Oh, God. She brought clenched fists to her chest, backed into the wall beside the stockings.

He was taller than she'd thought, he was leaner than she'd realized, he was closer than she'd ever thought he would be. And he knew about her showers.

She could smell him now. Not imagined steam, nor conjured soapy scent, but male skin heated by arousal.

He raised his hands to either side of her head, skated his palms lightly over her hair, the same way she did so often, back over her ears and down her nape as if he'd watched her and knew the gesture.

Then he leaned forward, his body still a foot from hers, and touched his lips to her ear. "I like your hair. The way you touch it." He inhaled slowly, an excruciatingly drawn-out intake of air. "And I like the way it smells. I'd wondered about that."

A shiver stole through her, from his warm breath on her ear, from his words, from the laying bare of his imagination. Arousal tightened her breasts, weakened her knees, stirred her body between. She caught back a whimper, the barest gasp at the back of her throat, closed her eyes and lifted her chin.

He could have her. All of her. She was that aroused. And equally frightened by a vulnerability that she wasn't used to feeling and didn't know how to fight.

Her skin burned beneath layers of knit dress and lace hose. Her muscles ached from the reflexive clenching and easing that came with each inch he leaned closer, each inch he halted, each inch he leaned in.

His body touched hers, barely; his chest grazed her breasts, barely; his thighs bracketed hers, barely. His shoulders rose; his stomach pressed into her belly. Fully.

He, too, was aroused.

She opened her eyes, looked into his, watched his pupils react as his hands left her hair to skim lightly down her neck. His palms grazed her shoulders, his thumbs pressed into her collarbone and her pulse jumped.

He felt it. She knew that by his eyes, by the flare of his nostrils, by the breath that fanned warm against her skin before his lips touched her cheekbone, traveled to her ear, worked lower. A wisp of air hissed from between her teeth.

He moved his hands down her arms, curled his fingers easily around her biceps, nuzzled his way from her ear to her shoulder. "I like the smell of your neck."

She raised her chin to give him better access, wanting to say something in return, but she couldn't find the words, couldn't voice the compliment she so wanted to return.

He smelled the way she loved a man to smell. His hair clean, sifting through her fingers as she held his head close. His face lightly spiced, nicely rough as his end-of-the-day beard grazed her jawline.

His hands were warm where they held her arms, his thighs hard against her hips. But it was the center of his body searing the center of hers that was her focus.

She could barely breathe.

He seemed to sense her dwindling control and lifted his head. Her neck cooled in his absence, but the heat in his eyes warmed her through.

"I like the way your eyes flash," he said. "I like to hear you laugh."

Oh, God. Oh, God. What was happening here? Her body was betraying her, responding to this man whom she didn't know at all as if she had known him forever.

She found him attractive, yes. Admired his dedication, of course.

And the fact that she was even attempting to inject logic into this moment proved how far gone she was.

So she gave up, gave in, raised up on tiptoes to better align his arousal with hers. He hissed. She whimpered. Her arms around his neck let him know he was welcome.

Nothing else mattered at this moment but his body and her body, and if he didn't put his mouth on hers and kiss her soon she was going to die.

So she kissed him. Not lightly as she should have this first testing time. Not gently as came with new beginnings. But as if she'd been waiting for this moment, this man, all her life. As if her survival depended on the touch of his mouth to hers, the breathing of his breath, the pleasure of this exploration, this discovery.

The kiss was more than she thought she would find, and she lost all patience, threaded her fingers into the soft hair at his nape and opened her mouth beneath his.

He kept his touch tender, more seductive than aggressive. The pads of his fingertips pressed the pulse in her neck; his tongue found the tip of hers and teased.

The moment began as a wild burst and settled into a precious thing, a holding, a touching, a mix of his breath and hers, his fingers on her neck, her hands in his hair, his lips and her tongue and two bodies reaching.

It couldn't last. It would never work.

She pulled away from the kiss she'd so wanted and

turned her head. He followed, learning the line of her jaw with his mouth, learning the curve she'd exposed, absorbing the texture of her skin, the nerves of her neck, marking with his tongue every spot that made her jump.

He made her jump.

It would never work. It couldn't last.

She turned her back to him, pressed her forehead to the wall, worked to catch her breath, to slow her pulse, to ease the fire burning from the tips of her fingers to the base of her spine.

His hands came up on either side of her head, flat against the floral-papered wall. Strong hands. Sure hands. Long fingers. Broad palms. Hands she wanted to feel on her body. Hands she wanted to lift her skirt from behind.

What is happening here?

"Isn't it obvious?" he asked and answered at once, pressing the front of his body into the back of hers.

She'd spoken aloud. "Yes," she managed to gasp, because it couldn't be more obvious than what she felt pressed to her back. "And it has to stop."

"Why?" he asked, keeping one palm flat on the wall, splaying the other on her stomach, not too low, not too high, just there, on her stomach.

She wanted his touch higher. She wanted his touch lower. She moaned. "We're standing in the lobby."

"No one's here. It's dark." His lips settled against her nape. "But we can go someplace else if you'd like."

"No," she blurted.

"No, we can go? No, you don't want to move?"

"Yes," she said, further confusing both of them.

His arm tightened around her waist. Ah, but she liked the way he made her feel, liked the way he felt, liked his touch, his breath on her neck, his fingers spreading wider.

She liked too much these things she had no business liking at all.

It couldn't last. It would never work.

"Yes, we can go? Yes, you don't want to move?" he asked, though how he could talk when his lips were making their way from one side of her neck to the other she didn't know. How she could hear anything but her heavy breathing, her heavy pulse, she had no clue.

She also had no will of her own, which left her as shaken as Duncan's touch. She didn't react this way to men. Not as a rule. Not ever. She wanted him, wanted to give herself to him, wanted both with a reckless abandon that was not Brooke Bailey.

His hand moved. Boldly. Upward. Covered her breast. Her breath deserted her, half gasp, half sigh, and she arched back against him. His hand moved. Boldly. Downward. Pressed low on her belly. Her hunger was as loud as the cry she couldn't contain.

"What do you want, Brooke?" Duncan asked softly, quietly, his voice a calm in her body's storm.

She wanted him to move, to let her go. She wanted things she didn't know how to ask for, things she needed to say no to. Things to send her climbing the walls. Things only he could provide.

She wanted relief. Release.

It would never work. It couldn't last.

What she needed was the return of her sanity. "Duncan."

"Mmm," he mumbled into her hair, pulling her back into his body.

She fought her longings and his hold to turn and face him with her back to the wall. "We can't do this."

"We are doing this." He slid his fingers down her jaw to her throat, his gaze focused on the movement of his hand and her response.

She arched her neck helplessly. "We have to stop."

"Whatever you say." He bent his head then and his mouth traced the path of his fingers. His tongue lightly dampened her skin, then boldly dampened her skin, then roughly left a trail of his making exposed to the warmth of his breath.

She felt close to panic. What did she say? What had she said? What was happening here and why couldn't she think straight and how did he know to press his tongue against that spot there on her neck and where was this leading and when would he stop?

Please don't stop. Please don't stop.

"That's what I thought you said," he said, and reached for the flippy ruffle of her skirt.

She gripped his shoulders. "Duncan."

"Hmm?" The ruffle skimmed her hips. His hands followed.

"Duncan," she repeated, her voice lacking the slightest note of conviction.

"Hmm?" The ruffle grazed her waist, his hands grazed the strip of skin between the top of her tights and her bra.

"Duncan." This time her words were panicked and aroused. Her body hummed, the pitch high and edgy. It was close to being too late. If she didn't stop him. She had to stop him.

Now.

She forced her dress down to her knees, pressed him back with her palms against his chest.

"Duncan, please. This isn't the time. Or the place." His heart thundered into her palm. "I'm not the right person."

His eyes flamed, then dimmed, then calmed at that. As if he knew and agreed and was as certain as she that things had momentarily gotten out of hand. That they'd return to normal along with her heart rate and his and they could go back to being friends despite this time out of time.

"Brooke," he said, and let her go, flattening his palms to the wall, his forearms grazing her shoulders. Barely.

She continued to look into his eyes, saw need and desire and a riot of confusion that had a footing in whatever had happened to make him a Grinch. "What?"

His eyes closed, opened. Searched hers. "Brooke. Kiss me. Please."

Oh, God. Oh, God.

He studied her reaction. Then waited. And waited. Until he was no longer able to wait. "I won't touch you. I won't move closer. I just want you to kiss me."

She never even considered saying no. He dipped his head just enough; she lifted her chin the same. Their lips met again, this time tender, this time that first time, the tentative movements and slow exploration.

He gentled her with his lips, briefly touched the tip of her tongue with the tip of his, ended a time that was all too short by placing a kiss on her brow. Then he stepped away.

He looked down at her with not quite a smile, not quite a frown, just a pensive look, a wistful look. Or maybe that flash of emotion he quickly extinguished could have been regret.

Brooke would never know. He wasn't her type; this never should have happened. It had, but it wouldn't go further or happen again. Emotional games weren't her style. Or his, she knew without knowing how or why. "Good night."

"Yeah," he said, touched the back of a finger to her face, then turned and walked away. He took the trash bag with him, bending to pick it up, then straightening and glancing overhead. Shaking his head, he reached up and slapped at the mistletoe the same way he'd slap at a pesky mosquito.

Brooke crushed the two turtle doves to her chest and closed her eyes.

"MAN, I HAVE REALLY screwed up," JJ said, his breath only slightly choppy for having run at least a mile.

Duncan really was going to have to find a new running partner. One who didn't talk so much. One who didn't get him into so much trouble.

Of course, this trouble was his own fault and had nothing to do with JJ or mistletoe, but with kisses that weren't kisses at all but extreme tests of his character and common sense—not to mention his *cajones*.

No, JJ might be the one complaining, but Duncan was the one who had really screwed up. "Then next time don't ask for my advice."

"Nothing wrong with the advice. Brooke's been having fun with the gifts." JJ laughed between breaths. "The five golden bagels was inspired."

The five golden bagels had come in a fit of frustration when Duncan wanted out of this bargain he'd made with himself to help JJ. Loyalty could be a real pain in the neck.

"I just hope she was hungry," Duncan said, and moved a step ahead.

JJ quickly upped his own pace. "The thing is, I don't want to stop with the gifts because I'll feel like a real jerk. But I don't want to give Brooke the wrong idea, either."

This was an opening Duncan had to take. For his own peace of mind, he needed to know. "It wasn't the wrong idea when you started."

They ran together, covering the next stretch of trail in silence. The winter sun was late rising, the early morning shadows cool, the air crisp. Enough dew remained on the running surface to add a damp squeak to the sound of their steps. It was a simple, uncomplicated hour of the morning, and Duncan didn't want to clutter it up with talk that required thought.

He preferred to remain in a brainless state where he didn't have to think about the clinic or the ER or the way he'd stood in his bathroom this morning dripping into the towel hung on his hips, his hands braced on the sink, his head hung low while Brooke's voice worked its magic on his body.

He hadn't moved while she'd showered, while she'd sung, while his hair had air dried and his body grown stiff. He needed this run. As much as he needed to hear the truth from JJ.

"You're right," JJ finally said. "At the time it was a great idea. I just hadn't thought it through."

"Why doesn't that surprise me?"

"No reason it should." JJ managed a panting laugh. "I still hold the Baylor track record for jumping in feet-first."

Again Duncan had to know and damned the need. Not that it would make a bit of difference, but... "You doing it again with Sally? Jumping without thinking?"

"You know, there are things you don't think about and should. Others you should think about and don't," JJ said and fell silent.

Duncan had nothing to say. He understood clearly what JJ had so simply spelled out. Brooke fell into the first category. Sally the second. The thought processes of the mind had no bearing over matters of the heart.

He knew that. Just because he was immune didn't mean he didn't know that. Just because he'd made the conscious decision to shut off his emotions didn't mean he didn't know that.

He made another decision now. "Don't worry about the gifts. I'll take care of it."

JJ glanced over. "You sure?"

"Where they come from won't make a difference as

long as they're impersonal and anonymous." And he would damn well see that they were.

"This should be a Christmas Brooke won't forget. Getting a jump on Miss Merry Christmas. I love it." JJ slapped Duncan on the back. "Thanks, man."

Duncan shrugged off the show of appreciation, made the turn for home at the usual place and wondered if a beer chaser would be inappropriate at six o'clock in the morning.

8

BROOKE SAT AT HER DESK in her Fielding-Lane office, going over the thematic proposals her staff had come up with for the first quarter of the year.

It was early yet. She knew that. But none of the designs that had crossed her desk were half as creative, half as thought-out, half as innovative as the Christmas gifts that had mysteriously appeared in her stocking each day for the past nine.

She'd come to relish the anticipation. To savor the moment of discovery. To prolong the entire process, walking repeatedly through the lobby, past the alcove, wondering if she should look now, if she should wait a little longer, until impatience and curiosity got the best of her.

For the first time in years, she was feeling the wonder, the magic, the miracle of Christmas. It lived not just around her but inside her, growing, blossoming, filling her until she felt the need to burst.

The work she'd done in the past to spread Christmas cheer had been rewarding; she'd loved the process, the results. She truly had. And if she'd given even a portion of the joy she was feeling now to any of the Baileys, her efforts had been fruitful.

This year, since she didn't have the madness of

Brooke's Bash to deal with, she'd turned her seasonal energy in another direction, toward her friends. What she could never have imagined was that she would be the one nearly brought to tears by the generous spirit of another.

These past days had been ones of discovery, rife with the dawning realization that the sense of home and belonging she'd always connected to family could be found with a feisty eighty-year-old matchmaker, an outrageously spirited blond girlfriend, an aggressive surgeon with career stars in his eyes.

But most of all, the connection she'd been missing all her life could be found with a Grinch who kissed like there was no tomorrow.

And that disturbed her. Immensely. She had no business feeling anything of any depth for a man she barely knew. A man she rarely talked to. A man who clearly considered her a Christmas pest.

A man whose passion in life was his career, who had no use for feelings. Brooke blew out an inelegant, unladylike snort. How could anyone have no use for feelings? Especially at this time of year?

Duncan's apathy toward the holiday was but a smoke screen thrown up to cover the depth of his emotional void. That was one of the things she'd come to understand.

She didn't want to think about the way she'd used her love for the holiday in a similar vein all these years. How she'd poked and prodded and bribed to get the busy busy Baileys together at Christmas.

And why? So that at least once a year she could pre-

tend what she had was the close-knit family she longed
for rather than a scattered lot of blood relatives?

Pushing off thoughts of the need to belong that she'd
never quite understood and pushing off more—
thoughts of times and holidays at home with Nanna,
the awakening appreciation of valued friends—she
shuffled through the proposals on her desk.

Which reminded her again of the gifts. As much as
the items affected her on a personal level, professionally she had come to admire the originality. Even taking into consideration her lifelong fascination with
decorating and love of all things imaginative, she
wasn't certain she could have conceived a concept so
extraordinary.

Not that the gifts themselves were unusual. Just
amazingly clever. Dinner for two at a local French res-
taurant on day three, which called for three French
hens. Four prepaid calling cards the next, to signify
four calling birds. She tapped a pencil on her desk and
smiled. The five golden bagels had made quite a lump
in her stocking. As had the six chocolate eggs—not
from geese, of course—wrapped in gold-embossed
foil.

By day seven she was certain she'd gained seven
pounds, and was thrilled to find the tiny, silver-filigree
music box that played pieces from *Swan Lake*. Day
eight had seemed a bit of a stretch, though if she
stretched just enough she could see the correlation between maids a-milking and the assortment of gourmet-flavored coffee creamers.

Day nine had offered an enigma. A note. Eight-and-a-half-by-eleven-inch white paper. Laser quality printing. Nothing incriminating in either. And no clues. Simply one word: *Patience*. That being day nine, it should have referred to nine ladies dancing.

Today was day ten. Brooke was out of patience. And she could hardly wait to get home.

But in addition to the palatable delights, as well as those aesthetic and practical and purely entertaining, each day's treasure brought her serious aggravation and grief. She wanted to know who was responsible. She had yet to rule out anyone.

Even Duncan.

She didn't think the gifts were his style. But then what exactly did she know of his style, beyond the way he kissed?

Oh, the way he kissed.

She drew in a huge breath, got to her feet and, arms crossed, turned to peer out the window behind her desk at Houston's Galleria. She thought about Duncan's style. Who he was. The way he closed himself off while proclaiming involvement.

She just didn't see how he could seriously separate one from the other. Especially since he wasn't as indifferent as he'd convinced himself he was.

It was the kiss that had told the tale. So much passion. And a big part of the reason she'd stopped him, stopped herself, when she had. The passion had held no meaning. If he had felt anything more than lust and bodily need for her, she could easily have taken him upstairs.

But Brooke didn't have sex, she made love. And it

took two people feeling to accomplish that incredible act.

So what she couldn't understand was why then, why now, why every time she saw him the thought crossed her mind? She didn't love him. She didn't even know him. But that didn't stop her from feeling.

Feelings that had no rational explanation. Which feelings rarely did. But at least she acknowledged hers instead of hiding behind the mask of a Grinch.

Duncan had once asked her about the motives for her actions. The question was one she wanted to turn on him. Why did he pour himself into his work if not to avoid his feelings? Why did he call what he did involvement when he wasn't involved at all? Why had he kissed her like he meant it when he didn't?

But the biggest question of all was one she needed to ask herself. One she needed to answer truthfully.

Why couldn't she get him off her mind?

At the brisk knock on her office door, she turned. "Come in."

Sally's froth of blond curls appeared around the corner. Her body, dressed in a slim suit of mango and kiwi, followed. "Busy?"

Brooke waved a hand over the sketches on her desk. "Busy waiting for inspiration."

"Would food help?" Long strides carried Sally into the room. She stopped in front of Brooke's desk and propped a saucy hand on her saucy hip. "Something rich and sinfully decadent?"

"It depends." Brooke looked her friend up and

down. "Are you talking about your outfit or chocolate?"

"I was talking about lunch. With me. And JJ. I'm meeting him at Carrabba's at eleven-thirty. Thought you might want to come along."

"I'm not sure," Brooke began. "Someone once told me three's a crowd."

Sally moped. "Ah, hon. I miss seeing you. Besides, three is a crowd only if the third is unwanted."

"Does JJ know you're inviting me?"

"You know he won't mind."

"He might." Brooke picked up her pencil, worried it from hand to hand. "I have a feeling JJ's a big supporter of two's company." The pencil stilled. "I've seen the way he looks at you, you know."

"You have?" Sally asked, her face taking on an ingenuous expression.

Brooke couldn't resist. "It's kinda hard to miss those big cow eyes he makes."

"Cows don't have blue eyes. Besides," she added, her look growing crafty, "that's a puppy-dog look. It sort of reminds me of the way Duncan pants after you."

Brooke's pulse blipped. She carefully placed the pencil on her desk. "Duncan doesn't have it in him to pant. That would require feeling. Besides, we've only kissed onc—" She cut off her own admission.

"You've kissed him? And you haven't told me?" Sally splayed both hands on Brooke's desk and leaned forward as nose-to-nose as she could get. "And what do you mean, he doesn't have it in him to pant? No, wait." She raised one hand, waved off her own question. "Start with the kiss. When? Where? How? I want details, Brooke Bailey."

Good thing Brooke loved her pushy friend. Otherwise she might have to hurt the woman. Teasing would have to do for now. "The kiss. Okay. With his mouth, in the alcove, on the second day of Christmas."

Sally growled. "Brooke, hon. This isn't a board game. I want more."

Brooke got up and paced a path behind her desk. "It was late. The night of the reception? I was cleaning up and he'd just come back from taking that emergency call."

"Did you catch him under the mistletoe?"

"Please." She stopped, glanced haughtily back over her shoulder and fought a grin. "I don't need cheap tricks."

Sally arched a brow. "Don't knock cheap tricks until you've tried them."

The grin escaped. Her friend's mood was nothing if not infectious. "Things with you and JJ that good, huh?"

"I can't believe how." Sally sat back in one of the office's plush blue chairs. "Why did you wait so long to throw us together?"

It was a question that Brooke had already tried to answer. "To be honest, until I saw the two of you in the lobby that morning, the thought had never crossed my mind."

Sally's expression grew pensive. "And why did it then?"

Brooke pulled her chair out from her desk, sat and kicked off her shoes. She tucked one foot beneath her and took her time picking a speck of lint from her hunter green trousers before meeting Sally's gaze. "I don't know."

Sally dropped both arms to hang at the side of her chair. "Great. I waited all that time for an 'I don't know'?"

"I know. I couldn't resist." When Sally stuck out her tongue, Brooke laughed. "You've been awfully sassy lately."

"I'm going through my second childhood. Or, in my case, experiencing the teenage years I was too grown-up to enjoy the first time around."

"You're having fun with JJ."

Sally sighed and fairly melted into the chair. "The best time of my life."

"Then what you're living definitely can't be the teen-age years." Brooke studied Sally's glow. "You're miss-ing the righteous angst, though maybe the walking, talking hormone part of it is accurate. Are you blush-ing?"

"Me? Blush? I hardly think so," Sally said, her color deepening.

Brooke couldn't help herself. "Then it was that good, wasn't it?"

Sally nodded. "And you get nothing more from me until you ante up a bit of information of your own. I want to hear about Duncan."

"There's not much to tell."

Sally lifted a perfectly patient brow. "You can start with the kiss."

Hadn't everything started with that kiss? "It was unexpected."

"The best ones usually are," Sally said.

And Brooke came back with, "On which you would no doubt be an expert."

"I wasn't until recently."

"Neither was I," Brooke admitted. "Until recently."

Until recently she'd never been kissed as if she was a man's only hope. And that such a kiss should come from a man she barely knew, a man who barely knew her, a man who'd closed off his feelings from the world...

That it should come from Duncan when he was so far removed from the place she'd been trying to reach all her life...

Nothing made sense to her anymore.

"So now it's my turn to ask."

Brooke looked up. "Ask what?"

Sally grinned. "Things with you and Duncan that good, huh?"

"Yeah. Better than that good. Which I just can't figure. I mean, there's really no reason that it should be. Better. Than that good," Brooke added, when Sally's expression grew increasingly disbelieving the longer she talked.

"Brooke, hon. What does reason have to do with anything?"

"Apparently not much. I feel so...out of control." It was a feeling she was having trouble resolving. It was complicating her life, consuming her thoughts, and she didn't like sensing she'd lost all discipline.

But she couldn't stop it and wasn't sure she would even if she could. And that just went to prove how out of control she actually was.

Sally mused, "Hmm. Out of control. I'd say that's a fairly accurate assessment."

"How can you stand it?" Brooke cringed at the grating sound of her own high-pitched voice. She strove for a level and less hysterical tone. "You never have a hair out of place. You coordinate your fruit-flavored suits, for crying out loud."

"This thing?" Sally asked, glancing down. "It was the talk of cabana boys the other day that made me do it. Totally inappropriate December wear, I know. But it fits my incredibly sunny mood. Want me to let you in on a secret?"

"Oh, please, yes." Desperately, Brooke buried her face in her hands. "Anything has to be better than the thoughts I'm having about this tasteless stuff coming across my desk."

"Is it really that bad?"

She shrugged. "My judgment is so clouded I can't even tell if I have any these days. Judgment, that is. My taste is fine. I think. I mean, at least I'm not a walking ad for the tropics in mid-December. Not that the idea doesn't have a bit of marketing appeal—"

"Do you want to hear this or not?" Sally interrupted.

Brooke was taken aback. Had she really been rambling? Pressing her lips together tightly, she nodded.

"I am in such an incredibly good mood that I can't stand myself."

"You can't stand yourself and you expect me to be able to? Through lunch?" Brooke cast a skeptical look in Sally's direction. "Well, maybe for Italian."

Sally laughed. "You're as demented as I am."

"Don't you think this is proof positive that women should avoid men? They drive us insane."

"But doesn't insane feel wonderful?"

What felt wonderful was Duncan's mouth, Duncan's hands, Duncan's body pressed to hers. Brooke suppressed a shudder. "It feels something, all right. I just wish it didn't."

"Why not?" Sally's frown echoed her confusion. "It's like being a teenager again and having a crush and not being able to think of homework or housework—" her expression grew pensive "—or anything but..."

"JJ?" Brooke filled in when Sally let the sentence trail off.

"Yes. JJ. I've known him two years, Brooke, but until the last few days I haven't known him at all. Now I feel like I've known him forever."

Why did Sally's illogical logic make such sense? And sound so familiar? "I think that insanity you mentioned is rearing its ugly head."

"See what I mean?" Sally crossed one leg over the other and swung it. "I was on the phone with Dr. Howard earlier. When I went back to review my notes of the conversation, I found I'd doodled JJ's name all over the legal pad."

"With a Mrs. in front of it?"

Sally nodded.

"That's light years beyond insane, Sally."

"I guess you haven't done it."

"Of course not," Brooke said, telling the absolute truth. "No reason to. If and when I'm ever a Mrs., it won't be to Duncan's Mr."

"You know that for sure?"

Did she know anything anymore? "As sure as I know that I'm going to be hiring an entirely new staff if these hotshots don't show a bit of the imagination they were recruited for."

"So, come to lunch. Get your mind off work."

It wasn't work she needed to get her mind off of. "Sure. Why not. As long as there is no talk of Christmas."

Sally's eyes widened. "You? Brooke Bailey? Don't want to talk about Christmas?"

"Today I don't even want to think about it."

"The gifts are getting to you, aren't they?"

Brooke glared. Sally didn't have to know how often and in how many ways the gifts were getting to her. "Did I just say I didn't want to talk about it?"

"We're not at lunch yet," Sally said, then stuck out her tongue.

Brooke rolled her eyes. "Okay. Starting now. No talk of Christmas. Better?"

"Until when?"

"Until I say so."

"Oh, now *that's* a mature response if I've ever heard one."

Brooke laughed, then strove for another equally mature response. "So sue me. But wait until after lunch. I suddenly decided I'm starving."

"I SWEAR WOMEN WERE put on this earth to drive men insane."

Duncan looked across the width of the doctor's lounge to where JJ lay sprawled on the institutional green vinyl couch, one arm blocking the overhead light. "You've finally figured that out, have you?"

JJ lifted the back of his hand from his near eye. "Nah, I figured it out a long time ago. Just not to what degree."

"Sally, huh?" Duncan asked, determined to keep the conversation on JJ's love life and not his own—which wasn't a love life at all, but merely an obsession.

And the height of insanity.

JJ's hand dropped back over his eye. He sighed. "I can't believe this has happened so fast. Whatever *this* is."

Duncan pushed the Brew button on the coffeepot and watched the steam begin to rise. Steam like that in Brooke's shower. It reminded him of the way she smelled.

He remembered her scent. Soft and tempting, a fragrance that fit her as perfectly as had that red dress. Both played a part in his unrest of late. An unrest that was doing its damnedest to make him feel.

"Are you two dating?" he asked, when the silence got too loud and the only sounds he could hear were the hiss of the coffeemaker and the uproar of his thoughts.

"Yeah. I guess you could call it that."

Duncan glanced toward the couch. "So, you're going out. Socially."

JJ swung his legs around and sat up. "We've been to dinner and lunch a few times. A couple of movies. The theater once."

"All that in less than two weeks? And you 'guess' I can call it dating?" At JJ's look of increasing perplexity, Duncan shook his head. "Is this exclusive?"

"I'm not seeing anyone else."

That sounded like exclusive to Duncan. "Do you want to? See anyone else?"

JJ thought a moment, raised one hand to rub the back of his neck, then scrubbed both over his face. Duncan turned back to the coffee. This looked like it was going to take a while.

At least he didn't share JJ's dilemma. He could state unequivocally that he and Brooke weren't dating. What he couldn't do was say that she occupied any less of his thoughts than Sally obviously did of JJ's.

Okay. He had a dilemma of his own.

"No. I don't want to see anyone else."

Duncan poured his coffee, knowing the way this conversation was headed he'd be wanting a beer chaser. Soon. "You sure?"

JJ's confusion cleared. His expression took on a sense of calm. "For now? Yes. I'm sure. Definitely sure."

Duncan took a swallow of the coffee, then said to his friend, "You feel better now? Or still insane?"

"Oh, I'm definitely insane. If I wasn't I would have nothing on my mind but the board appointment."

"Maybe work is all you should have on your mind," Duncan said, not sure which of them needed the advice.

"It's strange to say this—hell, to feel this—but having Sally to think about—"

Duncan cut him off. "Don't do it, Jay."

"Don't do what?" JJ asked, getting to his feet.

"Let yourself get distracted from your goals."

"Who said anything about losing sight of my goals?"

Duncan shrugged and brought the plastic cup to his mouth. "It's your concentration. You decide how to divide it."

"I really don't think that's a conscious decision." JJ laughed. "Just part of the insanity, you know?"

When Duncan continued to study his coffee, wondering when he'd lost command of his own concentration, how he could manage to get it back, where Brooke Bailey fit into the scheme of things, JJ stepped in front of him.

"Duncan. Don't worry. I've known for a lot of years exactly what I want to do with my life. I won't be distracted."

Duncan drank and JJ went on. "But I might be less likely to burn out if I don't have to make this trip alone." He looked Duncan straight in the eye. "You might want to think about that." He took a step toward the door, then stopped. "So, tell me about the gifts. How's all that going?"

"Nothing to tell. Three more days and it'll be done,"

Duncan said. He had no intention of getting into this with JJ.

JJ may have sensed Duncan's mood because, hands on his hips, he nodded. For way too long, he nodded. As if stirring up thoughts Duncan wouldn't want to hear.

Finally, JJ came to some sort of decision, and Duncan breathed a sigh of relief when all his friend said, "Well, I'm outta here. I have a date for Italian with a really hot blonde."

Then JJ slapped Duncan on the back and was gone.

Duncan watched the door ease shut and decided he hated coffee. It was bitter, acidic and did nothing but heighten nerves already strung tightwire taut. He felt the cutting edge, the bite, the tension waiting to snap.

Bottom line. He was feeling. Which wasn't supposed to happen. He hadn't made his third-grade vow lightly. Even at that very young and innocent age, he'd been old and cynical.

His teachers had labeled him hard to reach; the other kids called him stuck-up. Except for JJ. Who at the beginning hadn't cared about anything but the fact that Duncan could wallop a baseball, not to mention catch every one of JJ's wild pitches.

That common bond of baseball had started a friendship that had continued on through track and football, college and women.

But before all that, before career choices and bad relationships, back when nothing mattered but slamming the ball over the left-field fence, JJ had been the one to see beneath the surface of "that troubled Cox kid," to realize the only one cheering Duncan on when he got up to bat was JJ's own father.

The Coxes—Duncan's parents—had been cheering on other children. Ones who used concrete parking lots instead of ball fields, spray-painted squares instead of canvas bases. Ones who didn't have a left-field fence. Or shoes. Who didn't even know if they had parents to watch them play. Duncan's idealistic parents had tried to fill that void.

And Duncan had had Carolyn and David Mackey to fill his.

JJ's parents had helped Duncan endure school plays and *Animal Farm*, cleaned up more than one bloody nose and explained to him the good his parents were doing. Duncan tried to take the Mackey's advice and learned, at least, not to let his parents' commitment to others get to him.

He didn't let anything get to him. And he'd done all right for himself.

He still did all right for himself. Giving to others as the Mackeys had given to him. His work was rewarding, the involvement easy because he kept it impersonal. He no longer even wondered what it might be like to feel. To have involvement come from emotion rather than from his head.

Or at least he'd felt that way—thought that way, dammit—until Brooke Bailey decided to make him her Christmas charity case.

An interesting sort of full circle he'd come, from being abandoned for charity's sake to being courted for charity's sake.

Was Brooke Bailey courting him?

The unexpected thought jolted his system. Either that or he'd sucked down too much caffeine. The latter was more likely, he thought, pouring the dregs from his cup into the sink. The former meant...too much.

As if there was more involved here than Brooke's Christmas project. And that couldn't be the case.

Courting him would mean she was interested in Duncan the man. Not the doctor. Not the friend. What Brooke would want from him would require actions and reactions he'd put away long ago. So long ago, in fact, that even the memory barely remained.

How did one go about feeling things that counted? Things that required emotions. And risk. Things of the heart—and the soul.

He didn't know if he wanted to change. He liked his life the way it was. It was comfortable, it was safe, it was all he had ever really known.

He wasn't about to make himself over for a woman. Even though he knew—deep down he knew—that any change he made would ultimately be for himself.

Maybe one day. When he was ready. But not now. Not now. Not at Christmas.

Hell. Especially not at Christmas.

9

THE FIRST THING Duncan saw when he walked through the front door on the tenth day of Christmas was Brooke Bailey.

She stood toward the back of the alcove, set aglow by the tiny electric candles on the tree. It was enough illumination to accent the filaments of midnight blue threaded through the black of her hair.

Enough to highlight curves and enhance shadows and make him wonder again about what lay beneath the buttons of the oversize, plum-colored blouse she wore tucked into dark green slacks. He knew the texture of her skin, her smell, the feel of her hair even now pulled back with some sort of gold coil.

He'd never realized before that her legs were so long. Or that just seeing her from a distance could cause him to come to a dead stop. Memory of his discussion with JJ came back, as did the progression of his thoughts since.

What was she doing here messing with his life, making him think, making him feel? What exactly was she trying to accomplish?

And what was she putting in his stocking?

He leaned a shoulder against the alcove archway, crossed his arms and cleared his throat. She jumped, so intent on her task that she obviously hadn't even heard the front door. Unless she was faking it. Which he didn't think she was.

He liked that about her. That level of concentrated intention. The way she put her all into what she did. It made him wonder...

One hand pressed to her heart, she turned, discreetly tucking the other hand behind her back. Her blue eyes flashed with mock anger. "Don't you know it's not nice to sneak up on Santa's helpers?"

He fought a grin, wasn't sure he'd won the battle when he felt one side of his mouth lift. "Santa? I thought you were Miss Merry Christmas."

"Cute," she said, and smiled oh so very sweetly.

He scraped the sugar off his shoes and stepped into the room. She squirmed and stepped back. He stopped, lifted a brow. "Either I make you nervous or you have a secret."

"Of course I have a secret," she said in a huff. "It's December 22. Duh."

"Funny," he said, and made a gimme motion with his hand. "Let me see."

Eyes wide, she said, "No way."

"Yes way," he answered, and she vehemently shook her head.

She almost had him laughing. Almost, but not quite. One of these days he needed to figure out exactly why this woman set his blood racing. For the moment, though, he would enjoy it. For the moment he would feel. But only for the moment.

"I thought Santa didn't stuff stockings until Christmas Eve," he finally said.

She tucked back a strand of hair with the hand not hidden behind her back. Then she lifted her chin. "Santa doesn't. His helpers can do whatever they want."

"You don't say." Hands at his hips, he let his gaze drift to the row of stockings lined along the strip of paneling bisecting the wall. "Seems we have an over-abundance of Santa's helpers around here."

And just as he'd expected, Brooke wasn't about to back down. "You can just put away that Grinchy attitude of yours because I'm not listening. There's nothing 'over' about the abundance at all."

"Just your normal average abundance then."

"And you have a problem with that? An abundance of Santa's helpers?" She smacked a palm against her forehead. "Oh, wait. I almost forgot who I was talking to."

He walked closer, nonthreatening, yet with a purposeful air of false intimidation. "You're awfully sassy for someone backed into a wall with one hand behind her."

Her chin came up higher. "Are you threatening me?"

"Forgotten who you're talking to again?" he asked from as close as he dared get without recklessly stealing another kiss. Advance and retreat were a part of the game they were playing, a game that had begun with that first intimate contact.

"No. I haven't forgotten at all." Her saucy teasing faded away; her free hand came up to touch his face.

"Good," he said, pleased she hadn't forgotten, pleased that she'd touched him.

Displeased with his own pleasure, even as the beginnings of arousal beat a slow pulse through his veins. He had trouble keeping his own hands at his waist, when he wanted to touch the fingers so lightly running over his face.

He remembered touching her, what it had meant to him to touch her, the way she'd let him touch her. That was what he remembered. What he had trouble letting go.

"Are you all right?"

At her softly spoken question, at her hand sliding from his face, he looked up. "Fine. Why?"

She lifted one shoulder. "You looked...lost. In thought. I wondered if you'd had another bad day. At the hospital."

"No. My day was fine." She had come to his mind way too often. He acknowledged it and would work on the whys later. When she wasn't standing so close. When he wasn't itching, aching to touch her.

Hell, when *wasn't* he itching, aching to touch her? He caught back only half of the laugh that spilled from his throat.

"What's so funny?"

"Nothing. Me." He took a deep breath. "You."

"All of the above at the same time?" She pursed impudent lips. "Must be a strain for someone so in control of himself."

"You think I'm in control?"

Both hands were behind her now and she leaned back on the wall. "You think you are. I suppose that's all that really matters."

"I think I am." He considered that for a moment. "That implies that I'm not."

A careless shrug lifted her shoulder. "I wasn't meaning to imply a thing."

"Then what were you meaning to do?"

Uncertainty flickered in her eyes. "You were thinking about me. And you. In the same thought."

Uh-oh. "And you're looking for meaning in that?"

"Is there one?"

He didn't want to hurt her, but had to say, "I think we both know there's not."

"You're right, of course."

Her expression wavered, with relief or disappointment, he couldn't say. Didn't want to examine the implications of, either. Because for some strange reason he'd expected something different, something more.

"So turn around."

He looked up. "What?"

She made the motion with her hand. "Turn around. I need to finish doing my Santa's helper thing."

He turned around where he stood. Too close. She planted her palms at the small of his back and pushed.

"Move," she said with a grunt.

He did, but barely, fighting the smile her exasperation pulled from his lips.

"Santa's helpers have a lot of sway with the jolly old

soul himself," she said. "You're walking a fine line between this naughty and nice stuff."

Surrendering, he gave her all the room she wanted, which put him back in the alcove archway. He leaned a shoulder against one side, singularly avoiding the mistletoe still hanging in the center.

No way was he getting close to the stuff with Miss Merry Christmas in the same room. That one kiss had damn near been his undoing. It was insane that one kiss should affect him at all, much less jeopardize everything that had earned him the nickname Dr. Grinch.

"That's better," she said from behind. "Santa will be pleased."

"I doubt he cares one way or another. The big, red-suited guy and I have never had much of a relationship."

She was silent for a minute, the only sound in the room the shuffling of her stocking-stuffing movements. Then she unleashed a long, weighty sigh, and Duncan braced himself for what was coming.

"Have you had much of a relationship with anyone in your life, Duncan?"

Miss Merry Christmas, hell. Miss Nosey Christmas was more like it. "Sure, Brooke. JJ and I have been friends for twenty-seven years. I'd call that a relationship."

"But not with your family?" she asked, her voice a bit muffled since she faced the wall behind him.

"I have parents," he said grimly.

"No brothers or sisters?"

At that he had to laugh. "Blood relatives? No. But an

amazing number of fostered ones. My parents had, still have, a near religious calling to do for as many others as they possibly can in their combined lifetimes. I always thought they took the sentiment of the Golden Rule too far and forgot the mores of tending to their own household."

"You've been on your own a long time then."

He wouldn't bore her with the details. "Didn't take me long at all to realize I was all I needed."

"Everyone needs someone else."

That's where she was wrong. He stared out into the lobby proper, at the deacon's bench, the etched-glass front door. "Not everyone."

"Then you're a stronger person than anyone I know. I could never hold in my feelings the way you do. I have to have someone to vent them on. Or share them with."

Discretion was the better part of valor. "Sounds like a female thing to me."

"No, Duncan," she said softly, her movements slowing until the only sound in the room was the gentle release of her breath. "It's a human thing. You can turn around now."

He would; he just wasn't sure he wanted to. Right now, she was too close to him physically. Too close to him...deeper—emotionally. He turned around anyway, wiping the unrest from his expression. "Finished?"

She nodded.

"So I can peek?"

One blue eye narrowed dangerously. "Not if you want to live."

He shoved his hands in his pockets and smiled. He still wanted to touch her. And he didn't want to ask what he was about to ask. But a tiny vulnerable part of him needed to know more about her. And Christmas. "Did you stuff your own stocking, too?"

She considered him a moment—his question, his eyes—then took the steps to the tree at a slow, thoughtful pace. Her small laugh, when it came, held more self-deprecation than humor. "I didn't have to today. I have a Santa's helper of my own, remember? But I used to. For quite a long time."

Interesting. "Even when you were a kid?"

"A teenager, yes."

"Why?"

She fingered one of the ivory-colored bows fastened to the tree. The movements of her hands were telling. He wondered if she knew that—that she seemed to think with her hands.

"Family get-togethers were never a big deal with the Baileys," she finally said.

That surprised him. "Except at Christmas, right?"

She stood taller, as if preparing to defend her turf. He started to tell her he had no plans to start another holiday argument, but she went on.

"Christmas wasn't any different. Until I made it different. I was the one who wanted to live the Hallmark fantasy. Nanna—my grandmother," she explained with a wave of one hand, "knew that. She was the only one who did. The only one who cared."

He wanted to know more, but didn't want to interrupt again, so he crossed his arms and stayed where he was, watching her tactile exploration of the ornaments on the tree.

The motions were nearly hypnotic. He wondered if they helped her settle her thoughts, wondered why they had so easily calmed and settled his.

"Nanna helped me," she said, touching a fingertip to the point of one candle. "The celebrations started small, but grew to a fairly grand scale over the years. It came to be known as Brooke's Bash." She briefly glanced his way. "Sally may have mentioned that."

He nodded.

"It's funny, but just the past few days I've realized that all that time and effort was more for my own sake than anything. Don't get me wrong. I loved it and don't regret a bit of it. But I thought I was doing it for the Baileys. I wasn't."

He wasn't equipped to reply. Couldn't give advice, if advice was what she needed. He wasn't even sure how to offer comfort if comfort was what she could use. He did the only thing he knew he could do.

And as he drew closer, stepped in behind her, placed his hands on her taut shoulders, a weight lifted from a part of him that had been anchored there for a very long time. She leaned back into him, naturally, comfortably, and he was glad.

"They were always so busy, my parents," Brooke said, bringing up one hand to clasp her fingers with his. "Never home for holidays, birthdays, school happenings. They could have been, I guess. And I wouldn't begrudge them their careers...."

Her sentence trailed off and Duncan stiffened.

"I loved them dearly. They provided well. I never wanted for anything material. And if I needed more, well, there was always Nanna."

"You miss her, don't you?"

Her fingers tightened. "It's to be expected. This is the first Christmas..."

Her silent stoicism got to him more than female tears ever could, more than he'd ever thought he could be gotten to.

He turned her around, dropped a kiss on her brow, a brief one on her lips, and said, "I think...what you need...is to check your stocking, Santa's Helper."

She looked up, eyes suddenly bright. "What do you know about my stocking, Dr. Grinch?"

"Same things everyone else around here knows."

"Nothing more?"

He gave her a truthful answer. Just not the entire truth. "Maybe a bit more, but only because I know JJ and JJ knows Sally and Sally knows you."

"And the three of you talk about me behind my back, obviously."

"Isn't that what friends are supposed to do?" he asked.

Her smile returned. "Friends. Yes. I like that."

"So?" He inclined his head toward the wall. "Check your stocking already."

"Impatient?" she asked, and he thought of the note,

wondered if this was a test to see what he really knew, wondered how badly he'd just failed.

He waited. And waited. And just when he pretended to turn and go, she grabbed his arm and pulled him back.

"Okay," she said. "I'll check."

Again he waited, the knot in his gut a constant reminder of how glad he would be when day twelve was done with and they could both get back to their lives. If they could. After this.

When the plain white envelope came free of the stocking, he held his breath. When she lifted the flap, he exhaled. Her smile reached her eyes and held a large part of her heart. His own beat with unruly anticipation.

"This makes such perfect sense," she said, pressing the envelope to her breast. "Nine ladies dancing yesterday. Ten lords a-leaping today. How perfect."

Perfect. He could breathe again. Too bad he couldn't see straight. "What is it?"

"Two tickets to the ballet. The *Nutcracker*. For tonight." Mischief ran high when she met his gaze. "So, friend. You'll go with me, won't you?"

"I HAVE NO IDEA what to wear. What he's going to wear." Brooke shoved hanging clothes from one end of the closet rod to the other. This was ridiculous.

She should dress and be done with it. Who cared what he was going to wear? How gorgeous he would no doubt look in whatever it was?

Besides, she and Duncan had established their relationship as a friendly one. He wouldn't care what she wore. So why was she turning this into such a big production?

She moaned. Loudly.

Sitting cross-legged in the center of the floral-covered and gauze-draped, queen-size fantasy bed, Sally gave Brooke a thorough once-over. "Brooke, hon, this isn't the prom. You don't have to color coordinate with the man."

"I know." She pushed hangers to the left. "I'm being ridiculous, aren't I?" She pushed hangers to the right.

"I'd say you're being a perfect fourteen-year-old."

She finally took a black silk pantsuit from the closet and glared at her friend. "Fourteen? Ha! I'm at least sixteen and you know it."

Sally laughed. "So? This is a date? A date date? You and Duncan?"

The glare narrowed into slitted eyes. "Define date."

"Is he paying?"

Brooke stuck out her tongue. "Sexist."

"Well?"

"Unless he's my twelve-days benefactor, then no, he's not paying."

"You think he might be?"

Had she thought that? At least a dozen dozen times. Had any of those thoughts been serious? Not a one, she admitted, and sighed, returning the pantsuit to the closet. "Duncan? Hardly. I mean, why would Dr. Grinch give me gifts?"

"Why wouldn't he?"

"Sally, you're talking in geometry again."

Sally shook her head. "You're the one flying off on tangents and dodging the question."

"Which was?"

"Are you dating Duncan?"

Was she dating Duncan? Somehow they'd totally managed to skip that part of the male-female equation. They'd gone from acquaintances to friends to two bodies climbing the walls and each other.

They'd definitely left out a few of the steps. Which really had no bearing on the here and now. They wouldn't date because they had no future. And because they were just friends.

"Uh, Brooke?"

"No. I'm not dating Duncan. Friends don't date."

"Since when?"

"You know what I mean. Friends don't date romantically."

"Since when?"

Exasperation worked its way from her shoulders to her toes. "Forget it, Sal. We're not dating."

"So tonight isn't a date."

"No," Brooke stated emphatically. "Tonight is two friends going to the ballet."

"On a date."

Brooke growled.

Sally flopped back on both elbows. "Okay. I give up."

"Finally."

"But you two are so perfect for each other."

Brooke slowly turned, remembering how she'd had

the same thoughts of JJ and Sally. How she'd been right. "Why do you say that?"

"It's so obvious I'm surprised you would even ask."

"It's obviously not that obvious because I am asking."

A deep, thoughtful breath later Sally said, "I'm not sure I can explain."

"Oh, fine." Brooke slammed the closet door. "My curiosity is straining at the leash and you can't explain."

"If you're that curious you must be interested," Sally remarked, ending with a wiggle of both brows.

"In what you think? Didn't I just say that?"

"No. I mean interested in Duncan."

Brooke shoved her hands through her hair and pulled. "If I end up bald, it's your fault, you know."

"Those are your hands in your hair, hon."

"I know." Brooke flopped back on the pillows above Sally's head. "I'm really close to feeling something for him, Sal. Even though I know better."

"He's a good man, Brooke."

She thought of his dedication and commitment, thought of his dealings with Nettie. A good man. She didn't know if she'd ever known better. "Yes, he is."

"Brooke, hon, I don't mean to offend, but not everyone is going to be as gung-ho over Christmas as you are."

"C'mon, Sal. Give me a little credit. Christmas isn't even an issue. If it's anything, it's a symptom."

"Ooh. Dr. Bailey. I'm impressed."

"This isn't rocket science. Human beings aren't that exact, or predictable."

"Neither are relationships."

"I'm not predicting anything about our relationship." Of course, she couldn't predict what she didn't have.

"Except that you have no future with Duncan."

"That's not a prediction. It's a conclusion based on the available evidence. The man is married to his career."

"What about the unavailable evidence?" Sally asked.

Like how much of his upbringing Duncan was responsible for? How many adult decisions he'd had to make as a child? How often he'd felt the need to reach out, but had no one to whom he could turn?

Though he'd revealed only a fraction of his childhood, she'd summarily reasoned his parents had felt the need to parent elsewhere. He had felt the need not to feel, that being the easiest and simplest way to avoid being hurt.

Funny how he'd chosen a career that required more human compassion than any other that came to mind.

Yes, he was a good man. But he wasn't for her. She wanted a man who was unafraid to feel. Anything else was unacceptable.

"Brooke?" Sally asked.

"It doesn't matter, Sal. His dedication is to his career." Which meant family would always come second. If not third or even further down the ladder, she thought. She'd lived that as a child. She'd needed security, stability, a place to belong—and she still did.

But she'd also since discovered she could find that with friends as easily as with family. But most of it she could find within herself.

So why did a big part of her wish she could find it with Duncan Cox? Brooke sighed.

Then Sally sighed. "That leaves only one thing that does matter."

"And that would be?" Brooke asked, returning to the present.

Sally rolled over onto her stomach, propped both elbows on the bed. "Getting you gorgeous and to the ballet so that Duncan can see that being married to one's career isn't all that it's cracked up to be."

Brooke looked from her friend to the sheer panels hanging from the canopy frame above. "I don't want him to change for me, Sal."

"Of course not. Any changing he does would be for himself. But there's a lot to be said for being a catalyst."

"That seems to come with an implied responsibility. One I'm not sure I want."

"It only comes with what you want to give it," Sally said, tugging on a strand of Brooke's hair. "And, quite frankly, that's between you and Duncan."

"There's nothing between me and Duncan."

"And *that's* between your heart and your head."

Turning onto her side, Brooke faced her friend nose-to-nose. "You know, Sal, we're both getting way too deep in the psychology department."

"Comes from hanging out with these medical types."

Brooke grinned. "Is that it?"

"It's as good an explanation as anything."

"I kind of like the explanation that we're two bright, intelligent women."

"And independent and articulate," Sally added.

"And self-assured and way too savvy to use feminine wiles over wits and brains."

"Or savvy enough to know that those feminine wiles beat out machismo every time. Men are such men. Now..." Sally got to her feet, pulled Brooke to hers "...let's gussy up your wits and wiles and see what we can do about making Duncan go bonkers."

"You are a wicked woman, Sally White."

"And you love me for it."

"Yeah. I do," said Brooke, and gave her girlfriend a hug.

"Good," answered Sally, hugging back. "Because I love you, too."

SALLY WATCHED DUNCAN take Brooke's elbow as the couple walked out the front door. She sighed, wondering if this was what most mothers of teenage girls felt. It might not be the prom but it was close enough.

JJ snagged an elbow around her neck and pulled her close to his side. "Don't worry, Sal. I gave Duncan a good talking to. He'll have her home by curfew."

Sally elbowed JJ in the ribs. "Smart-ass."

"I'd say so."

"Oh, you would, would you?"

"Yep. Smart enough to get that board appointment I wanted."

Sally fell speechless. Then a huge smile spread across her face. This pleasure was totally different from what she'd been feeling minutes ago watching Brooke and Duncan practically drool all over one another.

She pulled back enough to look him in the eye. "Well, Dr. Hotshot. Can I say I knew you when?"

JJ used his elbow hook to drag her toward the stairs. She went along with his caveman tactics because she knew he had the heart and soul of a real man, a good man. Ten days' worth of late-night talks had seen to more than physical intimacy.

And one day soon she'd tell him that she loved him.

"You can do better than saying you knew me when," he said, returning her attention to the moment at hand.

"Oh yeah? How's that?" she asked, one hand around his waist, the other flat on his stomach as she walked by his side up the stairs.

"You can say you know me now."

This man was too much, and she wouldn't have him any other way. "How generous of you."

"Yeah, I don't have the big head just yet. I'm still your ordinary run-of-the-mill plastic surgeon."

There was nothing ordinary about J. J. Mackey, but then she knew he knew that. "So, where are you taking me, Dr. Hotshot?"

"You choose. Your place or mine."

"And what are we going to do there?"

He shrugged. "I figured we could watch TV. Wait for the kids to get home."

She forced a yawn. "I guess I can spare the time."

"Yeah?"

"Yeah. I always take a night off to celebrate after I get a new account."

He came to a complete stop, turned her to face him. Both his blue eyes and his dimples flashed. "You got the hospital account."

She nodded. "Think that place is ready for me to show Mercy?"

"I don't know about the hospital, but you can show me mercy anytime, Sally White," JJ said.

Sally decided her apartment was closer. Saving a few steps was the only mercy J. J. Mackey was going to get from her.

10

BROOKE TOOK THE STAIRS from the lobby to the second floor slowly for several reasons. The first one being the cut of her dress. Together, after half the contents of her closet ended up in a pile on the foot of her bed, she and Sally had decided on an oriental sheath.

The jade green silk was formfitting, the mandarin neck high; the sleeves capped her shoulders. The bodice was cut to accent, bisected by a placket fastened with tiny, fabric-covered buttons. The skirt was calf length and very very slim.

Walking required concentration. Climbing stairs required raw nerve. Especially with Duncan Cox so close behind—another reason she was making the trip up the stairs slowly. She didn't know if he was watching her walk. Not knowing made her nervous.

His hand lay at the small of her back. And he trailed her by only one step. Which meant more than likely that his eyes were straight ahead and not...where she'd prefer them not to be.

But more than affecting the wiggle in her walk, the slower pace would prolong her time with Duncan.

This evening had been magical. She wanted the fairy princess feeling to go on forever. And she didn't want her time with Duncan to end.

The man she'd sat next to at the ballet had not been the Dr. Grinch she'd come to know and love. Love as a friend, she clarified, though she knew that wasn't the whole truth.

She'd been wrong about him not feeling. Tonight, while sugarplum fairies spun across the stage, she'd sneaked surreptitious glances his direction. He'd smiled at all the right places, grown somber at others, been as moved by the music as she had. He'd let down that guard he carried so proudly.

And as arrogant as it might seem, she was going to take some of the credit for that.

Not that she had changed him. But as Sally said, she had been the catalyst, giving him options he might not have considered before. Showing him that feelings were essential to life. He relaxed more around her now than he had a month ago. He teased. He even flirted.

She knew she was walking a tightrope here. Nothing had changed when it came to Duncan's dedication to his career. And it shouldn't have. Not because of her. Not for her.

Yes, he'd rearranged his schedule to accompany her to tonight's ballet. He seemed to have done so willingly. And she hated to wrongly read too much into that. She wouldn't read too much into that.

Still, knowing what she was up against, recognizing what stood between them, she wasn't ready to let him go. Not so soon. Not yet tonight.

So when they got to her apartment door, she invited him in.

"Unless you have an early morning," she added to the invitation. "And need to get home."

"No," he said, taking her key from her hand. "I'd like to."

"Great," she said, and smiled before bracing herself with a deep breath.

She entered first; he followed and closed the door. The last time he'd been in her apartment they hadn't yet kissed. That knowledge, that memory, the passion they'd shared simmered, breathing an air of tension into the room.

The apartment was dark. A tiny bit of light came from the small appliance bulb over the stove. She flipped the switch to the floor lamp standing in the corner of the living room. That bulb blew.

"Sorry. I'll get a replacement," she said, tossing her evening bag onto the bar.

"That's okay. I'd rather have coffee."

That stopped her for a minute. "You'd rather have coffee than light?" When he nodded, she said, "All right," and went on into the kitchen, where she made coffee.

The stove-top bulb cast light far enough into the living area for her to see Duncan settle back into her big black pillow chair and square one ankle over the opposite knee. What she couldn't see were his eyes. But she felt them. And she stayed where she was—facing him across the open bar while the coffee brewed.

The aroma filtered through the air and she inhaled deeply. Yes. Duncan was there. That subtle male scent she knew to be his lingered. Whether from elbows and shoulders brushing in the theater, whether from his hand on the small of her back as they climbed the stairs, his scent surrounded her while he watched her from the other room.

She swallowed hard, thinking of all the reasons she needed to turn on the overhead light. Thinking that jade green silk did little to hide the effects of cold, less to hide the effects of arousal.

Why was she aroused when he hadn't touched her, hadn't spoken since they'd walked into the apartment, but for those few words requesting coffee instead of light?

There was no an answer except that he was Duncan. And that she wanted him...to kiss her again. To touch her as he had then, again.

She shook off the thoughts as the coffee finished brewing; shook off the fantasy as well. She'd serve him his coffee, then send him on his way. In two days Christmas would be over. She could quit playing Miss Merry Christmas. He would no longer be Dr. Grinch.

They would be just neighbors. Better acquainted than before the holiday, of course. And hadn't that been her goal, after all?

"How do you take it?" she asked, her voice huskier than she would have liked, but the timbre came with her mood. When he didn't answer right away, she said, "I have sugar, sweetener, low-fat milk. I even have eight gourmet-flavored creamers."

He still didn't say anything. But he moved. Stood. Seeming to take up all the space in her living room. She found it incredibly hard to inhale. When he walked toward her, fabric brushing fabric with each step, she found breathing nearly impossible.

He wore dark slacks, a dark sport coat, a collarless linen shirt of a shade slightly less dark. She'd met him in the lobby prior to the ballet and she still couldn't get that moment out of her mind. She'd always thought him gorgeous, but now, like then, she realized that his looks were made by the confidence he emitted.

His coffee-cocoa eyes glittered, and that single, shining light picked up every shade of blond in his light brown hair. Again she thought his coloring that of a bird of prey. And tonight she felt hunted. Especially with the smoky, hooded look he slanted her from beneath long lashes.

"Coffee's almost ready," she said, refusing to cross her arms for fear he'd take the move as defensive. Defensiveness implied fear, and she was anything but afraid. What she was was uncertain—as to the thoughts going on in his mind, as to where this evening would end.

He took up the space in her kitchen doorway, palms braced on either side of the arched opening. His jacket hung loose, the lines of his dress clothes accentuating his lean, runner's body.

She gripped the cabinet ledge cutting into her back to keep from exploring him as she wanted to do. She wondered if he would mind her need to touch, then quickly put the thought away before she did exactly that.

It was when she turned to retrieve two cups from the

overhead cabinet behind her that he entered the kitchen.

She heard him first, his steps on the tiled floor. She felt him then, close to her back, inches—or less—away. Smelled him as he leaned forward, his face a shadow's width from her neck. Saw both of his hands braced on the countertop at either side of her waist.

All that was left was to taste him. She shuddered with desire and the need for his mouth on hers.

"I've changed my mind," he said, his breath warm where it fanned her skin, his words low in her ear, his heart beating against her back. Or so she imagined, since he wasn't really touching her at all.

"About the coffee?" she asked.

He nodded, his lips in her hair, on the shell of her ear.

"I have tea," she managed to get out. "Diet soda. A beer."

He shook his head at each offer, aligning his body with hers as he did so. Her knees grew as weak as her resolve.

"I can't get you anything to drink?"

"Yes," he murmured. "But later."

Later? Did that mean he was staying? The night?

"Duncan?" she asked.

And he murmured, "Mmm?"

The vibration of his voice tingled along nerves steadily growing unbearably tight. "What are we doing?"

For a moment, then another, he stayed where he was, silently standing behind her. Too close for comfort, too far away for the same. "You have music?"

Music? She nodded. "The armoire. In the living room."

"Then we're dancing," he said. Wrapping his big hand around her wrist, which had never felt so small, he led her into the darkened living room.

Using the light from the stereo system she switched on, he chose one of the CDs she had stacked on the player. Then he took her in his arms, and when the music began, they danced.

She fit against him well. Her cheek rested on his shoulder, giving her nose and lips access to his neck. His skin was warm, his scent comfortably familiar. His shoulder was supportive, his hands strong. The sound of his breath and the beat of his heart soothed her only slightly less than they stirred her.

He was Duncan. And he was her friend. Nothing more. She had to remember that. And then she heard the music. "Christmas carols?"

"I thought you'd like it."

"I do. I didn't think you would."

"I can be persuaded."

She smiled into his shoulder. He must have felt it because he squeezed the hand he held and looked down.

"Music's easy," he said.

"It's a start, anyway."

He chuckled, deep and low. She felt the rumble through her breasts, deeper, through skin and flesh and into her heart. Oh, how she loved to hear him laugh.

He did it so seldom. He was selfish with his laughter, as if it was not to be taken lightly, but to be given sparingly, and only when deserved. It pleased her to be found deserving.

And she so enjoyed the way he moved, so fluidly. Enjoyed the way he held her, so possessively—or was it desperately?—with thighs and knees touching. The night was perfect and her senses were content.

She smelled the coffee. The light designer scent she wore mingled with the warm spice of his, the pine from her Christmas tree and the mulberry candles she'd burned earlier in the day.

She settled closer; he pulled her closer still, until she couldn't tell his breath from her breath, the pulse beating at the base of his throat from the equally heavy one thrumming through her body and her blood.

Her skin tingled with arousal where his hand held her fingers tightly against his chest, where the palm he'd splayed low on her back moved lower with each beat of music, with each step they took to each beat.

And somewhere between Handel and Tchaikovsky, between "Carol of the Bells" and "White Christmas," between her sigh and the low-throated *grrr* of satisfaction that resounded deep in his chest, she fell completely in love with her friend, Duncan Cox. Her cantankerous, curmudgeonly, caring, compassionate Grinch.

Snuggling her face into his neck, she kissed him lightly, the barest brush of lips to skin heated by her breath. That catlike sound of male satisfaction rumbled through his chest and Brooke trembled.

She hummed against his neck then, at first nothing but soft noises, her lips grazing his throat. When the music stopped, when the CD changed, when the next melody began, she whispered the words to "The Christmas Song," mixing the softly mouthed lyrics with an even softer murmur of the tune.

"I want to hear you sing," he said, his voice rough as if his throat was too swollen to speak.

Her feet faltered; her voice stopped altogether. "I don't sing," she said, knowing that she did, where she did, when he would have heard her.

"Yes. You do," he answered, and moved to put more space between their bodies than she wanted. He reached over, increased the volume on the stereo, then took her by the hand and turned.

She followed, knowing exactly where he was heading, where *they* were heading, what would happen once they got there. No, she had no idea what would happen once they got there. But she wanted to find out.

She pushed aside the tiny flurry of reservations her subconscious raised. This wasn't the time for thinking. This was the time for feeling. She wanted Duncan to sweep her away only slightly less than she wanted to take him to a place where he'd never been.

He opted for the hall light that filtered into the bathroom in a haze. It was enough. She could see the glitter of arousal in his eyes when he turned her to face him.

Reaching behind her, he untied the ribbon she'd loosely braided through her hair. The strands fell free, brushing her shoulders, framing her face. It felt strange. And then, when his fingers slid deep against her scalp, it felt totally wanton and wild. He kissed her, catching her lower lip between his teeth before he pulled back.

"I want to hear you sing."

She could hear the music coming from the speakers in the living room, but singing was what she did for herself, not for an audience. That this audience was Duncan complicated her dilemma.

He placed his lips on hers lightly. "Sing for me, Brooke."

How could she sing with his mouth so close? When all she wanted to do was kiss him?

She draped her arms over his shoulders, leaned into him to do just that. But he pulled back until no part of his body touched hers save his mouth.

"Sing. For me."

"Now?" she mumbled against him.

"Now," he said, and so she sang.

A word or two here. Another one there. She grasped at the lyrics drifting from the speakers in other room. The tune was one she could easily carry; the words escaped her scrambled mind.

But she soon came to realize what Duncan wanted more than anything was just to hear her voice. Off-key, it didn't matter. Missed lyrics, he didn't care.

He listened, eyes closed, hands in her hair, mouth learning the feel of the words that formed on her lips. What became important were the sounds she made. Her whispers. Her anxious moans. Her husky, throaty whimpers. He absorbed them all.

It was the sexiest kiss that wasn't a kiss she'd ever experienced.

And it only got better when Duncan released her, leaned over to turn on the tap in her tub. He picked up a bottle of berry-and-floral-scented shower gel, shot a stream into the running water. Bubbles frothed and the fragrance steamed upward.

Brooke could barely breathe.

Duncan shrugged out of his sport coat, draped it over the back of her vanity chair, loosened the top two buttons of his shirt, the top two buttons of her dress. He turned her around then, pulled her back into his body, forcefully lifted her chin.

She looked into the mirror.

Though the room was dark, their reflection was visible, his face next to hers, his eyes bright, hers brighter. He wrapped his right arm around her waist. His left hand went to the third button on the high neck of her dress. Went there and stopped.

The shadow of his beard was rough against her face. She rested one hand on the back of his at her waist, lifted the other to his hair, his temple, petting, stroking, drawing a hiss of satisfaction from between his lips where they lay at her cheek.

His reflected gaze met hers. "I know you can sing, Brooke. I hear you. Every morning. I set my clock. To get up. So I can hear you sing."

"I hear you, too," she whispered, arousal stealing through her in mad ripples and shivers. "Stepping in and out of the tub. I hear you pull the shower curtain. I hear your water run."

He started on the row of buttons then; worked them free, slowly. Flicked one from its fabric loop; moved to the next; continued until the bodice panels parted, opened, exposed her bare breasts, the centers drawn and dark against her pale skin.

Their eyes met in the mirror and she watched him watch her. His gaze dropped to her breasts, hers to the left hand he lifted to cup her right breast. He weighed her, molded her, tested her resilience.

And when his fingers pulled as his palm cupped, her body began to sing. She whimpered, softly at first, but his touch grew more insistent and the volume of her moans increased.

"That's it, Brooke. Sing for me," he said, stirring the fire in her body with his words, with his touch.

This was a song she could sing. Her head lolled back on his shoulder. This was new, never what she'd expected to feel, she thought as her arousal mounted. Never, never, never what she'd ever felt before.

Her body ached, wanting something she didn't know. Her eyes burned and she closed them tightly. Her heart beat as if it had just come alive.

Duncan placed his hands on her shoulders, pulled her dress off and down her arms. The silk skimmed her hips and, once he moved back and distanced their bodies, the material slid to the floor.

She stood before his mirrored reflection in nothing but a scrap of red Christmas satin and black platform heels. His eyes roamed intimately; his hands skimmed the same path, barely touching. The pads of his fingers deftly touched, explored, discovered every innocuous spot that brought her pleasure.

And oh, how he brought her pleasure, pressing here,

then there, drawing as much response as he could from each place before testing the next. All the while she watched his eyes as his eyes watched the movements of his hands on her body.

The eroticism of the moment was not lost on Brooke. A part of her detachedly witnessed Duncan making love to the woman in the mirror. The voyeurism aroused her, adding a hint of the forbidden to a moment that seemed to be stolen from time.

Yes, there were reasons he shouldn't be here, but right this minute she didn't care.

It was when she let go her inhibitions and went from impartial observation to wanton participation that Duncan's movements became more than the ones in the mirror, became the very skillful touches shortening her breath, stirring her blood.

And despite all her efforts to remain composed, she began to strain and sweat.

He splayed his fingers low on her belly above the elastic holding the satin close to her skin. She squirmed from the warmth, from the pressure, from the restless want for more. He gave her more, pressing the ridge of his erection against her scantily covered backside.

When she pushed her bottom to him, he groaned her name low in one ear. When she whimpered in response and wiggled harder, he growled like a man in pain. When she reached between their bodies with the fingers of one hand, measured his thickness, gauged his length, he fairly and wildly and abandonedly roared.

And then he retaliated, lightly scraping his short, blunt nails across her Christmas red satin.

She wanted those nails on her skin, wanted his fingers beneath the elastic. She craved feeling him without the restrictions of the clothing he still wore. And so she turned.

He let her unbutton his shirt, loosen his belt, pull the hem free and spread the dark linen. She looked up into his eyes as she lowered her head and placed her tongue at the hollow of his throat.

His chin came up. His breath rushed out. His heartbeat jumped beneath her open mouth. She lay wet kisses along his collarbone, from one shoulder to the other, as she pushed his shirt down his arms, trapping him in the dark, fabric bonds.

His skin was warm, the wedge of hair across his chest silky. She teasingly pulled with her fingertips, licked with her tongue. He panted harshly, shoved his hands in her hair and drew her face down his torso.

Wanting to please him, but thoroughly pleasing herself as well, she tasted the skin she'd exposed, learned the lines of his ribs, the indentation of his navel. And when she lowered his zipper she learned even more.

He sucked in a sharp breath, gripped her shoulders and let her have her way. He was an easy man to please, and the taste and smell of him aroused her unbearably. Her impatience grew, and sensing the change, he pulled her upright and flush against him.

The contact of her breasts with his chest dampened her panties. She skimmed her hands over his back, low enough to slide his slacks off his hips. He kicked out of his shoes, then out of everything else he still wore. Once naked, he made quick work of her panties.

Which was fine. She could always buy another pair.

She stood naked before him, wanting to touch and taste the body standing naked before her. But she couldn't glance away from his eyes. He had that look. Needy, yet vulnerable. And deep inside she felt the power of all she could give him.

She started with a kiss to show him her feelings, the tenderness of lips against lips, the passion of mating tongues. His arms came around her, his hands spread on her back, holding her to his proudly aroused body.

Then he broke contact, stepped into the tub, pulled her with him. He turned the flow of water from the tap to the showerhead, while she made sure the clear curtain was closed.

And then she had him, Duncan, there in her shower, water beating down on his head, making wet every part of him she'd imagined wet.

She smiled. He slicked back his hair and did the same.

"What?"

She shrugged, felt a rise of color to her cheeks. "I've imagined you in the mornings. In your shower. But I hadn't pictured you in mine."

"I didn't care about the shower," he said. "I just wanted to get you wet."

If he only knew. If he only knew. "I like the way you think," she said.

"Trade places with me," he said, looking down at

her, water streaming from his hair, the tips of his lashes, the end of his nose, his mouth.

"Okay," she whispered, a strange sense of hesitance stealing into the moment. She understood it, really. She was naked and he wanted to watch her. Any self-respecting female would've suffered the same reservations.

At least it was dark, which made it easier to ignore her imperfections. Though from what she saw in Duncan's eyes, she didn't have a single one.

She took a deep breath and brushed by him, her hands on his hips, his on her arms while, as he'd directed, they switched places. That tiny brush of skin to skin increased the tingles that kept the flesh raised into bumps on her body. Even the warm spray on her back failed to soothe.

Though was soothing what she truly wanted? To be soothed? Not if soothing meant a calm, quiet easing of the chaos churning madly beneath the surface, a lessening of her body's tempestuous storm.

No. She wanted to play out this fantasy. The one she'd lived for the past month, listening to Duncan's shower run above her. Imagining. Thoughts that had never, could never approach this fiercely keen reality.

The only thing that needed to be soothed was the ache burning in her belly.

"That's better," he said, as she smoothed back the wet strands of her hair. "I've wanted to see you like this, your hair wet, your skin..."

The sentence trailed off and so did his finger in a line down the center of her throat to the hollow where he traced the half-moon of her collarbone. The water ran warm and berry-scented bubbles foamed around her feet.

She leaned back, pressing her spine to the black and white ceramic tiles. The pulsing water spilled over her shoulder and onto Duncan's chest. He reached for the shower gel, worked the soap into her soft sponge and drew the lather in sudsy trails down her neck, her shoulders, lingering on her breasts.

With the supporting wall behind, she closed her eyes, listened to the fading strains of the music, the water rushing past her ear, the increasingly audible beat of her heart and Duncan's labored breaths.

His hand traveled lower, his palm cupped around the sponge while a single finger traced down the center of her torso, lower, stroked over her navel, lower, maddeningly lower, until she closed her hand around his hand and pleaded, "Duncan."

"Brooke," he answered, and all was lost. His mouth was on hers and his upper body pressed close to her soapy skin, and his fingers finished what they had started.

She couldn't take any more. This was beyond what she could bear. And so she begged. "Duncan, please."

He answered by aligning their bodies and reaching behind her to the backs of her thighs. He braced one foot on the corner of the tub, lifted her leg to drape over his.

Her arms went around his neck then and she kissed his throat, drinking the water that ran from his skin, his resilient, heated, smooth male skin. He tasted of warmth and more, things she couldn't put into words.

She never had a chance to try.

He pulled back to look in her eyes. "Ready?" he asked, and she nodded.

He entered her. Slowly. Pushing deeper, deeper, his gaze locked with hers every inch of the way. Her breath caught as he filled her. Completely. And then he withdrew and began again until the strokes of his body met the thrusts of hers.

The tempo increased, their rhythm metered to the pounding of the water, the rush of blood through their veins, their hearts.

She wanted to look away, to feel, to experience his power without the distraction of his eyes. But something in his gaze refused her. She couldn't look away.

Even when he slid a hand between their joined bodies, used a finger to speed her response, pressing where she most wanted to be pressed, using the water and the lingering suds to heighten the carnal seduction of his touch, she couldn't move her gaze from his face.

Even when the first stirrings and tingles and shivers tightened her body, when the moisture he used came not from soap and water but from her, when the part of him inside of her swelled her and stretched her and swept her to the edge, she couldn't close her eyes and hide.

But he knew. That look of greedy male satisfaction told her he knew, he felt, he wanted to see. His desires were her undoing. She let go, gave in.

And Duncan watched her come.

11

HE NEEDED TO LET her sleep. And he would. Later. As soon as he'd filled himself with her completely.

Feeling the sweep of Brooke's deep, even breaths at his shoulder, Duncan stared overhead at the filmy fabric draped in intervals along the white iron canopy frame. The strips of lace and gauze seemed randomly placed, but he knew the effect was the exact one she wanted.

He knew that about her. That she was careless about nothing. A part of that was the artist in her. The rest was that she didn't have it in her to be anything but attentive. To decorating details, yes. But even more so to the friends she kept close.

He couldn't help but wonder what it would be like to be more than a friend, to be cared for, by her, always.

But since he couldn't have always, since he shouldn't even think about always, he would take tonight. Take her again. Until she could take no more.

And then, when he'd pulled himself together, when he was sure he'd left nothing of himself behind, that was when he would leave.

He would think about tomorrow tomorrow. Right now he wanted to think about the feminine width of

Brooke's shoulders where she lay sleeping on her stomach at his side.

He turned toward her, propped his head in one hand and, with the fingers of the other, lightly measured the span of her back, her shoulder blades, the length of her spine, the swell of her hip, her bottom.

She shivered, snuggled closer, turned on her side. He pulled up the sheet and tucked her to him like a spoon. She was warm. His arousal was immediate and centered in need for this woman.

The feel of her skin against his was an aphrodisiac. Her scent filled his mind. He pressed his lips to the curve of her shoulder and remembered her taste.

He let go of all thought and surrendered to his senses then, to the desires of his body, the draw of where he knew she could take him. Of where he could take her, wanted to take her.

Gently he returned her to her stomach, leaned over and marked her, at first with tender kisses across her nape. Then, as she responded, circling her hips, whimpering low in her throat as she came awake, he made his need known with broad strokes of his tongue on her skin, opening his mouth low on her back.

She roused and whispered his name, worked to turn to face him. He refused her that freedom, but gave her the rest of what he'd learned she liked, what she craved, what drove her wild.

He wanted to drive her as wild as she drove him, to balance the power he quickly felt slipping from his grasp. Control wasn't the issue. But the need to retain his sanity, his sovereignty, burned as strongly as his desire.

At least until he raised over Brooke completely and she lifted her hips into his groin, moaned and breathed out one word.

"Please."

He wanted to enter her then from behind, to nudge her knees wide and settle his hips over hers and slip his arm beneath her soft belly, pull her as tight to his body as the fit of man to woman would allow.

But he wanted her more face-to-face, her stomach, her breasts pressed against him. So he turned her. Then he covered her. And felt all of what he wanted to feel. The skin. The softness. The breath she spent against his neck.

She sighed in surrender and he entered her—slowly, to allow her to adjust, to draw out the moment, that first sensitive stroke as he buried deep. He shuddered, held himself still, absorbed the feel of her.

It was when he began to move that he absorbed more. The scent of her arousal as her skin grew slick, her movements manic to match the reckless speed of his. The rake of her nails down his back. The clutch of her fingers into his hips. Her need for him almost matched his need for her.

His need for her was strong. He'd only known one stronger in his life—one need, resulting in one vow.

But as Brooke moved beneath him, as her urgency increased, as her body changed to accommodate his, swelled in enjoyment of his, he came to know more.

That in this moment, with this woman, his vow had been broken. Irrevocably.

And any problem he'd thought he had was nothing compared to what he'd face in the morning.

Because he had fallen in love.

DUNCAN THOUGHT that by dressing in the bathroom, where he'd left all his clothes anyway, he could avoid waking Brooke. He was wrong. By the time he'd put on all but his sport coat and headed for the front door, she was in the kitchen and coffee was ready.

He didn't detour from his course. Not because he was avoiding her, but because he needed to get to the hospital. And he didn't want to be fooled by the air of domesticity he sensed in the making.

An air that implied things like...caring, like interest and attentiveness, when none were really necessary. Yes, he and Brooke had had a night of great sex. If he kept it in those terms, kept anything resembling emotion from the equation and, above all, kept at bay that moment of weakness he'd had in the middle of the night, it would be easy to leave.

It was when he thought about how much more he could want with her, how close he was to giving in to his feelings—dammit, yes, his feelings—that leaving became difficult. He couldn't take a chance and stay. The risks to the comfortable level he'd worked a lifetime to reach were too high.

Duncan blew out a deep breath, attempting to relieve the tension that held his chest tight. He ignored the pounding in his head. He deserved that much discomfort, at least, for acting like the bastard he preferred she think he was by leaving this way the morning after.

Though he would, and did, stop on the opposite side of the open bar long enough to say goodbye. He wasn't *that* much of a bastard, after all.

"Would you like coffee?" she asked sweetly, her face scrubbed clean, her hair a sexy, unkempt mess falling to her shoulders.

He'd never seen her so disheveled before and liked knowing he was the cause of her wantonly debauched appearance. He shifted where he stood; shifted, as well, his debauched train of thought.

"I'd better get going," he said. "I'm on duty—" he glanced at his watch "—in an hour."

She tightened the sash of her dark purple robe, a color she wore often and wore well. The satin folds clung to curves he knew intimately, curves he wanted to know better. Again. Now.

He had no business wanting anything more when it came to Brooke Bailey. Because she was something he would not let himself have.

"Yeah. I need to get to the store." She brushed back her hair. It tumbled again over her shoulders.

This time she left the strands where they fell, as if using the curtain of black to shield her reaction to his departure. Her attempt to hide came too late. He'd seen disappointment dull the blue of her eyes. The pounding in his head doubled.

She poured herself a cup of coffee. "Christmas Eve. Last day of the crazies."

He wanted to bury his hands, his face, deep in her hair, her neck, the center of her body, and inhale the way she would smell of their mingled scents. "At least until the twenty-sixth, right?"

She laughed. He loved the way she laughed. "Oh, yeah. Everything that was either the wrong size, the wrong color or the wrong style will be returned with a vengeance." She made a face. "'I already have this one. I want that one instead.' 'The one I received is broken. Can I have a replacement?' 'This clashes with everything in my house. I'd like a refund.'"

She shook her head, rolled her eyes. "It never ends. The one part of the hustle and bustle I'll admit to not liking."

The commercialism he'd decried earlier. Still... "You mean there's a part of Christmas you actually don't like?"

"Only a small one," she said, measuring an inch between forefinger and thumb. "And I'll take it as long as I can have the rest." She shoved her hands in the deep pockets of her robe and sighed. "This really has been a great year."

Duncan heard her words, but saw more. The implication in her eyes that he had more than a little to do with the quality of this particular Christmas. A part of him liked that. A lot.

Another part of him didn't want to take credit. He had no stake in the outcome of her holiday season. He needed to remember that, to convince himself of that.

But the biggest part, a part he kept deeply hidden, a part he'd for years denied existed...that part thought about the future, the possibility—even the promise—of future great years with this woman.

Exhaling deeply around the knot in his stomach, Duncan took a step back, shrugged into his jacket. "I'd better go."

She nodded, gave him that content-female smile that had hearth and home and commitment written all over it. "Thank you. For the ballet."

"Sure," he said, thinking that he liked that smile a lot, when he shouldn't have liked it at all. "It was a nice evening."

"Yes. It was." She stepped closer, though the bar still kept them separated. "You need to do that more often, I'm sure."

If she was talking about the ballet specifically, he'd have to disagree. If she was talking about taking the time to enjoy himself, well, that bore consideration. He'd ignored pleasure for quite a while.

But if she was talking about the hours between midnight and four, hell, yes, that was something he needed, wanted to do more often. And he wanted to do it with her. As much for the way she'd made him feel in the shower as the way he'd felt after, lying in bed, holding her.

He shuddered to think how bad it would feel when he didn't have her to hold. "I don't know. I think that was enough culture to last me awhile."

She laughed again. His gut knotted again. He reached for the doorknob.

"I'll see you?" she asked, her voice tremulous for the first time.

"I'm sure you will. I live—" he pointed toward the ceiling "—up there."

"I know."

"Okay, then," he said, and not knowing what more to say, opened the door, closed it behind him, leaned back, closed his eyes and breathed deeply.

When he looked up, it was straight into the eyes of Nettie May. She wore a gauzy scarf on her head, a Pepto pink quilted housecoat that reached her calves and matching slippers with fuzzy fur cuffs.

She also wore a disapproving expression and held a gaily wrapped package that matched the ones on the floor in front of both Terri's and Sally's doors.

"Whatever happened to tradition?" he asked once he found his voice.

She narrowed one eye, pursed her lips, didn't say a word.

This was going to be a grilling the likes of which he'd never had in his lifetime. Funny thing, but he felt he deserved it. *Well*, he thought, and frowned, *maybe a part of it.*

"First Brooke stuffing stockings and now you delivering packages. Both before Christmas morning." He clicked his tongue. "Santa is going to have your hides."

Her other eye narrowed further than the first, until it was a wonder she could see through the slits. "Santa is going to have to wait."

"For?" Duncan raised a brow.

Nettie parked a bossy hand on her hip. "For me to get through tanning yours."

"Think you've got it in you?" he tossed back, enjoying the spark that flashed through the octogenarian's squinting eyes.

"Oh, I've got it in me, young man." Her bossy hand became a bossy finger shaking in his face. "You'd better have an explanation for being in Brooke's apartment this time of the morning."

"I was making a house call?"

"With only three buttons done on your shirt and your belt hanging halfway out of your jacket pocket and your hair looking like it hasn't been combed with anything but your fingers?"

He leaned forward, whispered in her ear. "They weren't my fingers, Nettie May."

"Oh, you—you scoundrel," she said, and smacked him in the center of his chest.

He caught her hand. "Don't worry. I didn't hurt her," he said, even as Brooke's hesitant last words came back to prick his conscience.

Nettie considered that, considered him, came to a conclusion. "You haven't *yet*," she said, then gave him no chance to reply. "Do you know what today is?"

"Sure. December 24. Christmas Eve."

"And?" she prompted.

"Wednesday?"

Nettie took his chin in her hand and pulled his face to her level. "The eleventh day of Christmas."

Uh-oh. "And that's supposed to mean something to me?"

"It means that you'd best decide what to do about eleven pipers piping before that young lady in there checks her stocking and finds it empty."

He strove for innocence. "You don't think—"

"I don't have to think. I'm eighty. I *know*," Nettie said, then left Brooke's package on the floor before her door, left Duncan standing in the hallway alone with his thoughts.

He watched her make her way down the first flight of stairs to the landing, thinking he might need to increase her arthritis medication, that he didn't like the way she was favoring her right knee, that she was full of way too much spit and vinegar for five o'clock in the morning.

And that he had absolutely no idea what he was going to do about eleven pipers piping.

BROOKE SHOULD'VE WAITED until after work to check her stocking. But it was the morning of Christmas Eve and she was feeling the anticipation infecting Christmas lovers everywhere.

She assured herself that was all she was feeling. That holiday jitters were the source of her anxiety. Not disappointment over finding her stocking empty. Or Duncan's early departure.

At least he had said goodbye.

He could've walked out without a word. Which might have been his game plan had she not caught him in the kitchen. She wasn't sure what she'd wanted to accomplish the morning after. A reassurance of sorts, she imagined. That she didn't expect declarations of...anything.

She was still too caught up in the events of last night

to know what she expected. Or wanted. Other than Duncan.

Why did mornings after have to be this hard?

"Brooke, dear. Don't you look Christmassy this morning." Nettie's voice came from behind, and Brooke turned to see her landlady stepping into the alcove, a kitchen step stool tucked under one arm.

Brooke briefly glanced down at the Christmas-tartan trousers and pine green poet's shirt she wore. "It seemed appropriate wear for the day." She touched her fingers to the ornate angel brooch pinned over the top button at the collar of her blouse. "The pin is gorgeous, Nettie. Thank you."

Nettie tilted her head one way, then another, admiring. "Just making sure my girls know they have someone watching over them." She raised all-seeing, all-knowing eyes to Brooke's face. "Making sure they don't get into any...trouble."

The emphasis Nettie put on the word *any*, not to mention *trouble*, told Brooke she hadn't imagined hearing her landlady outside her door with Duncan this morning. "And it's nice to be looked out for."

"Well, you never know what type of scoundrels and scalawags you'll find roaming the halls in the wee hours."

Brooke thought of Duncan's deep brown eyes, his light brown hair streaked with blond, thought of him wearing all black as he had last night. Then she thought of him wearing nothing. In her shower.

She shook off a shiver that ran from the roots of her hair to curl her toes in her shoes. "And what would you know about scoundrels and scalawags wandering the halls in the wee hours?"

"This is my building. And I make sure the only scoundrels and scalawags roaming these halls are decent ones."

Was Duncan decent? Nettie seemed to be concerned and waiting for an answer, so Brooke responded to the question they'd both raised. "I don't think you have anything to worry about."

Nettie went about unfolding the step stool in the center of the archway. "That's the second time I've heard *that* today," she mumbled.

Brooke wondered if her landlady had been referring to Duncan and if Brooke herself had been meant to hear. Then she realized that Nettie was climbing, unaided, onto the second step of the stool. Brooke hurried forward.

"What do you think you're doing?"

"Since the nibbles have slowed, I thought I'd move the bait to the front door," Nettie said, reaching for the mistletoe. "See what other fish I can catch."

And then she took a misstep. The stool buckled, slipped on the tile. And Brooke screamed as her landlady fell into her arms and tumbled with her to the floor.

DUNCAN WAS STANDING at the nurses' station in emergency when a nurse walked Brooke through the wide-swinging electric doors. He did a double take, dropped the chart he'd just marked into the desk assistant's hands and hurried down the corridor.

Blood rapidly soaked through the gauze pad fastened above her left eye. *What the hell*, he thought, his heart pounding out a heavy bass beat. That much blood and no doubt she'd need stitches. He could manage, but he'd rather have JJ. Duncan tried to remember if his friend had said anything about his schedule today.

Brooke had stopped and waited while paramedics rolled a gurney through. She brushed off an EMT's attempt to replace the soiled bandage and turned her frantic attention to the individual on the gurney.

Duncan frowned, looked that direction. And realized the person on the gurney was Nettie May. Damn.

A flurry of activity, rapid-fire questions and answers, and Nettie was on her way to the X-ray department, while Brooke was assigned to a treatment room, her vitals taken over loud objections that she was fine, that it was Nettie who was injured.

"She's being seen to, Brooke," Duncan said, walking into the room, her chart in his hand, noting that her pressure and pulse were within a normal range.

She looked his way for the first time then, and at the sight of her red-rimmed, swollen eyes, he tightened his grip on the folder in his hand, determined to remain detached. To get to the bottom of whatever it was that had happened. To see that this remained a doctor-patient encounter and nothing more.

To make sure he didn't let what was proving to be one hell of a tension headache interfere with his judgment. Or her treatment.

He laid the chart on the examining table behind her

and reached for the bandage on her forehead. "Why don't you tell me what happened."

She winced as he probed the skin surrounding the wound. "Nettie fell."

"Down the stairs?" he asked, cleaning dried blood from the edges of her wound. The cut was nasty, but clean. Easy enough to stitch. Still...

He shook his head and argued with himself that he wasn't showing preferential favoritism, but opting for the best treatment for this patient. He turned to the nurse assisting him. "Michael, would you locate Dr. Mackey for me?"

Michael looked from Duncan to Brooke and back. "Dr. Mackey?"

Duncan nodded. Decisively. "I want him to take a look at Miss Bailey's forehead."

"On my way, Doc," Michael said, though Duncan detected the unspoken question of principles in the nurse's tone.

So be it. Duncan would answer for his decision. He turned back to Brooke. "Well?"

"No. It wasn't the stairs." Brooke finally answered his question. "She fell from a stool. And why do you want JJ?"

He looked at her like the answer was obvious. "I want Jay to stitch up your forehead. I could do it, but I don't know if you want to go through the rest of your life looking like Frankenstein's monster."

She smiled a bit at that.

"I'm kidding, of course," he said, disinfecting and lightly dressing the tear. "But this is JJ's specialty."

"JJ's a surgeon, Duncan. These are just stitches."

"Humor me, Brooke," he said, and stepped back, shoving his hands into his pockets. He was going to throttle her if she questioned him again. "If he's busy, he'll let me know. Now tell me what happened to Nettie. And to you."

She folded her hands resignedly in her lap. "I was on my way to work. I'd stopped in the lobby to drop a few gifts under the tree. Nettie climbed up to move the mistletoe."

"Climbed up on what?" Duncan asked, bracing his hands against his hips.

"A step stool."

His heart thumped. "And you let her?"

"She was halfway up before I even turned around and saw what she was doing. And, yes, then I tried to stop her." Brooke shook her head, remembering. "It looked like her knee caught. Or gave out. The stool slipped. And we both went down to the floor."

"And this cut?" He lifted his chin, indicating her forehead.

She gingerly touched the dressing. "From the stool. A bolt or a sharp edge. I'm not sure."

"When was your last tetanus shot?" She shrugged and he reached for her chart and ordered the injection.

"Aren't you going to check on Nettie?"

"As soon as she's back from X-ray, yes, I'm going to check on Nettie." Duncan added his notes for JJ. "What was she doing messing with the mistletoe, anyway?"

Brooke sighed. "Something about moving it. Wanting to catch more fish."

He thought a minute, then shook his head. "Guess she got a little too caught up in your Christmas cheer." And even as he said it he felt Brooke stiffen, throw up a defensive, impregnable shield.

"My Christmas cheer?" She arched a brow, then winced when it was the wrong brow. "I wasn't the one who put up the mistletoe."

"No, but if you hadn't hung the stockings and decorated the tree, she wouldn't have felt the need to contribute, would she?"

"Are you blaming this on me?"

"It's just circumstances, Brooke."

"Circumstances that are somehow my fault."

"It was an accident. Let's leave it at that."

"An accident you're somehow trying to blame on Christmas."

He wasn't. But it probably wouldn't hurt to let her think so. The fact that they'd slept together hadn't changed a thing about who he was. She needed to realize that he was still the unfeeling workaholic that he'd purposefully made himself into.

"You can think whatever you want," he said. "It doesn't change the fact that Nettie fell moving Christmas mistletoe in the lobby that you decorated."

The look Brooke gave him had sent better men to hell.

"You know, Duncan," she said, just as JJ walked into the room. "I always thought that compassionate, caring, feeling people made the best doctors. Know what? I was right, Dr. Grinch."

"YOU FEELING BETTER?" JJ asked, handing her coffee in a disposable cup. Brooke gave the brew a skeptical look and JJ laughed. "It's from the doctors' lounge. I promise it's safe."

"It really doesn't matter. I doubt I'll be able to taste a thing." She touched her cheek. "This entire side of my face feels like putty. My mouth like a bale of hay."

"The anesthetic will wear off soon enough. It's what you're going to feel tomorrow that'll take longer to get over."

"I'm going to feel your stitches?" Brooke asked, then tried to sip the coffee. That was easier to concentrate on than the other things she might feel tomorrow. The main one being that last night had been a horrendous mistake.

She wasn't naive enough to think that one encounter would accomplish a one-hundred-and-eighty-degree change in her relationship with Duncan. But after her earlier run-in with Dr. Grinch, she felt like a cheap bumper sticker. Save Water. Shower with a Friend.

"A bit," JJ said, bringing Brooke back to the present. "But not as much as the muscles and ligaments and whatever else you bruised when you fell on that lobby floor."

Brooke crossed her legs beneath her and sat back on the hard, vinyl, waiting-room couch. "I'll be fine. It's Nettie I'm worried about."

"Duncan's keeping her overnight for observation. A bit of an irregular heartbeat. Nothing to worry about. She'll be fine." JJ shook his head. "Not so much as a strained muscle. You must've broken her fall."

"What a crummy Christmas Eve. If only I'd seen earlier what she was up to."

"What? You think you could've stopped her?"

"Yes. I do." No matter what Dr. Grinch thought. And no matter what Dr. Grinch thought, Nettie May was going to have the Christmas Eve she deserved. Brooke perked up. "Will they have Nettie in her room soon?"

"It might be a while. Mercy's a bit short staffed this evening."

"JJ, can you give me a ride home?"

"Sure. You could use a good rest."

Brooke eased up to her feet. "I'll get one."

And she would. Later. After she'd done what she had to do.

HIS SHIFT HAD BEEN long over when Duncan stopped by Nettie's room before heading home. He'd checked on his landlady earlier, even after the resident assigned to her case had assured him there was no need, that her vitals were stable, that she was resting comfortably.

Duncan didn't bother to try and explain that there *was* a need. He was still working through that one himself.

Because as detached and impersonal and doctor-to-patient as he'd tried to remain, he was well and truly involved. From the mind, yes. But equally so from the heart.

There. He'd admitted it. He was feeling. His concern for his landlady—his friend—went way beyond the boundaries of professional ethics.

Soon enough, he was sure, he'd get to the multitude of emotions he'd refused to acknowledge for the biggest part of his lifetime. When he did, he'd take them one at a time.

For the moment, the sensation of being vulnerably exposed was enough to deal with.

As were his feelings for Brooke.

She'd been in Nettie's room; he saw that the minute he pushed through the wide door. He inhaled deeply, exhaled slowly, yet still found it hard to swallow for the tightness in his throat. Everywhere he turned, everywhere he looked, he saw Brooke.

Her influence. Her work. Her passion for life. Her love. There wasn't a single part of him that didn't feel the connection. *That* was how involved he was. How involved he wanted to be.

How much he loved her.

In that moment, with that admission, the cold wall in his chest splintered, cracked, fell away. Warmth thawed the last of the ice around his heart, which expanded to contain all he felt for this incredible woman who had come into his life when he'd most needed, least expected, to find what he'd been missing.

A warm smile spread over his face, spread deeper into his very soul. He savored the feeling and the moment, knowing his future had just been defined.

He glanced first at a soundly sleeping Nettie, then around the dimly lit room at Brooke's handiwork. Miss Merry Christmas had left her mark and left it well.

In the fringed throw of reds and greens woven into a scene of Santa and his elves that covered Nettie's faded blue hospital blanket. In the string of blinking lights hung in a square around the coldly sterile window. In the candy canes and multicolored balls hooked over the wiring at every third light.

In the quilted tree skirt draped over the seat of the visitor's chair, the one-foot ceramic tree with painted ornaments centered on top, the three brightly wrapped packages stacked at its base.

He wasn't at all surprised by her efforts. Even with

the fall she'd taken, the trauma resulting from the gash JJ had neatly repaired, even with the adrenaline-rush exhaustion that he hadn't doubted had set in, she had taken the time to see to Nettie's needs. Needs that couldn't be met by Mercy's overworked staff.

This was the essence of who Brooke was, her strength of character. And so much a part of why he loved her.

Rolling the day's stress from his shoulders, he lifted his gaze from the three small packages and turned to the window. The lights blinking above his head caught his eye. Made him wonder more about Brooke's attachment to Christmas, the family at home that hadn't seemed to care, the undertaking she made this year on behalf of friends.

Whatever the root of her need to expend time and energy spreading holiday cheer, the upshot was that this issue went way beyond Christmas. This was about finding her place.

She hadn't closed herself off from the chance of further hurt as he had, but had reached out to do for others, unselfishly offering what she herself had never had. She had taken chances, risked her heart, searched for happiness, refused to settle.

She had played Santa and stuffed stockings for a group of people who otherwise would have felt the sting of a holiday spent alone. She had planted a seed of romance between two friends and watched JJ and Sally's love blossom. She had nurtured an elderly woman who had no family of her own, giving Nettie a new sense of direction and purpose.

And he had done nothing but balk at every attempt Brooke had made to draw him into her circle of friends, into her very heart. He had been a hell of a fool.

No longer. Now he wondered if it was too late for him. If Brooke's heart was big enough to still want him. If he could open his enough to deserve her gift should she find him worth loving.

Because he definitely found her so.

"Our girl sure brightened up this place, didn't she?" Nettie's sleepy voice came from behind him.

Our girl. He liked that. Turning his back to the window, he asked, "What are you doing awake?"

"Watching you," Nettie answered, seemingly amused, as if he'd done something she approved of.

Duncan crossed his arms to get serious with this one. She needed her sleep. "Watching me do what? Check on you?"

"Have you done that?"

"I'm getting around to it."

"I thought you might." She scooted up in the bed. "Once you finished checking up on yourself."

"You think that's what I'm doing?" Duncan asked, moving forward to plump the pillow at her back.

"I'm eighty. I know."

"You're eighty. You had a bad fall. You need to be resting."

She shook her head and worked her mouth into a petulant sulk. "I want to stay up and wait for Santa."

Duncan refused to encourage her by laughing. He cast a glance at the three presents beneath her tiny tree. "I think Santa's already been here."

"My Santa, maybe. What about Brooke's?"

Uh-oh. Duncan closed his eyes and cursed himself.

"You didn't forget, did you?"

"I forgot."

"Then you'd better hurry home and do something about it," Nettie said, flinging a box of tissues at his midsection in an obvious display of eighty-year-old pique.

He watched the box hit first his stomach, then the floor. "I'm sure she's already checked her stocking. It's too late."

"It's still the eleventh day. It's not too late," she said, and he had a strange feeling she was talking about more than today's gift.

"How am I going to come up with anything between now and midnight?"

"I don't know." She shook that bossy finger his direction. "But don't forget at midnight it will be day twelve. A day of miracles."

Yes. At midnight it would be Christmas. "You get to sleep. It's the only way you're getting out of here tomorrow. I want you to be home for Christmas."

Nettie settled back down in the bed, bossy finger and all. "My, my, Dr. Grinch. That's about the nicest thing I've heard you say since I've known you. I'm glad to see that you've settled things with yourself."

He inhaled deeply. "I'm not sure they're all settled. But I'm getting there."

"You'll do fine." She looked at him then, eyeing him first one way, then another, focusing at last on a place beyond his shoulder. A place separate from here and now. "You know, since my dear Walter passed on, Christmas has been difficult for me. I've listened to others sing carols, watched them share loving times with their families. And I've grieved.

"But this year Brooke refused to let me wallow in the past. She helped me create new memories. A tiny miracle, considering how stubborn I am." The wry gleam in her eyes intensified into a laser that probed his innermost secrets. "Christmas miracles can happen, Duncan. All you have to do is open up and let her in."

"We'll see," he managed to answer huskily, and leaned down to drop a totally unprofessional kiss on her cheek. "Now sleep."

She burrowed deep beneath the Christmas throw he pulled to her chin. "Scoot," she said, waving her hand. "You have an eleventh and twelfth day to take care of, Santa. And now that my job's done I can sleep."

"And what job would that be?"

"Oh, nothing," she said, then murmured, "I always knew that mistletoe works in mysterious ways."

Shaking his head, Duncan headed for the door, stopped, looked back to see her gray eyes smiling his direction. "How did you know the gifts in Brooke's stocking were from me?"

She smiled a beatific smile. "I'm eighty. I know."

"I'M OKAY, Sal. Really." Brooke settled back on the deacon's bench in the apartment lobby late on Christmas Eve.

Sally tapped an imperiously maternal foot. "You need to get to bed and sleep."

"I don't want to sleep. I want to wait up for Santa," Brooke said, and laughed at the frown Sally delivered. "C'mon, Sal. It's almost Christmas. Let me be a kid a little while longer."

"All right," Sally said, and sat down beside her, tugging on the hem of the short black skirt that slid halfway up her crossed thigh. "But only if you promise to grow up *and* get to bed once the big red guy shows."

Even though Brooke laughed, she wasn't going to promise a thing. Not to someone who had the legs to wear a skirt as long as nothing.

And not if growing up meant that she couldn't enjoy Christmas and life, that she'd become a Duncanlike Grinch and never feel. No thank you.

She relished her inner child too much. Relished all that she was feeling. She could even deal with the disappointment and regret she felt over Duncan. Later, when the pain wasn't quite as fresh, she would deal with the reality that he hadn't returned, or wanted, her love.

At least being miserable meant she was alive. That she hadn't locked herself away because of the Baileys' emotional abandonment.

The security she'd craved from her family was here, among her friends, would be there among future friends for the taking—as long as she continued to give freely of her heart. The love she received in return was the essence of family, after all.

Yes. She'd be fine. More than fine.

She'd so wanted to give the same contentment to

Duncan. But deep down she knew he'd have find it himself, just as she had.

She looked over as Sally smothered a yawn.

"You go on up," Brooke said. "I'm fine. I want to sit here awhile and enjoy the tree and the music."

"I wish you'd come with me," Sally said as she got to her feet. "You can sleep over. I'm going to stop by JJ's for a bit. He said he had something to give me. But I shouldn't be long."

As tired as she was, as bad as her head hurt, Brooke couldn't help herself. "I'll pass on the sleep over. Besides, what JJ wants to give you might take all night."

"Brooke Bailey!" Sally said, and blushed.

"What?" Brooke asked, mock aghast. "I just meant that not all Santas deliver at the same time."

"What about your Santa? What happened to day eleven?" When Brooke shrugged, Sally said, "No gift?"

"I figured it was Nettie. I just hope she doesn't worry about missing the last two days," Brooke said just as the front door opened. She looked over to see Duncan walk through, his face weary, his solemn expression directed inward.

Oh, God. No. Brooke's heart raced. "Duncan?" she called to get his attention. "Is it Nettie?"

He looked up, bypassed the staircase and headed toward her. "She's fine. Why?"

"You look worried." He looked more. Exhausted and weary and fighting an internal battle. Oh, how she wanted to ease his burden, to rub the exhaustion from his shoulders, to care for him, to love him right out of his somber mood.

But she didn't have the right, would never have the right, and her throat tightened in response.

He shook his head, shook off his distraction, shoved his hands in his pockets and smiled. "I was just... thinking."

Brooke wanted to ask, decided to let him tell her in his own time, his own way. If he wanted to tell her at all. Or not, if this war was one he needed to wage and settle alone.

Sally saved her from asking anyway when she leaned down and gave Brooke a hug. "I'm going to run. But I'll see the two of you later."

"Night, Sal." Brooke returned her best girlfriend's hug and her heart swelled. How fortunate, how very, very lucky she was to have Sally in her life.

"Merry Christmas, hon," Sally whispered, then waved her fingers and trotted up the stairs, leaving Brooke alone with Duncan.

He sat on the edge of the far end of the bench, leaned his elbows on his knees and looked over. "Is that what people wear while they wait for Santa?"

She felt the quirk of a grin on her lips and glanced down at her reindeer slippers, eleven-pipers-piping socks and the knee-length sleep romper that could easily have passed for the costume of an elf. All she needed was the hat.

Instead she'd let her hair hang loose. "I like it," she said, and her chin came up. She wasn't going to argue with the Grinch.

So when he replied, "I like it, too," her heart gave a little lurch of surprise, then sped up with foolish hope.

"How's your forehead?" he asked.

She tested the edges of the bandage. "Sore. But manageable. JJ prescribes great drugs."

"So Nettie always said," Duncan replied.

"She is going to be fine, right?"

He sat back then, laced his fingers together in his lap and stretched out his legs. Brooke's gaze was drawn to their length. She remembered their feel against her own and sighed.

"She's a tough one," Duncan said. "I knew her arthritis had flared up. I should've increased her medication a while back."

Brooke blinked hard at this turn in the conversation they'd had earlier today. "You're not blaming yourself for her fall, are you?"

"No. It was an accident. I doubt additional medicine would've helped. Or you turning around any sooner would've mattered. She had her mind made up that she was going to move the mistletoe. It doesn't matter what any of us would've told her to do. She's eighty. And—"

"She knows." Brooke chimed in on the end, sharing as well a warm smile of affection. "She's such a sweetheart. I'm glad I've gotten to know her."

"Yeah. I am, too."

Again his comment took Brooke aback. "Are you all right, Duncan? You seem..."

"Out of sorts?" he asked.

"No. Just tired, I suppose."

"I am that. I'm also regretting what I said to you today."

"Don't worry about it. You just explained."

"Thanks," he said, and fell silent.

She didn't want him silent. She wanted him talking, explaining the things she'd heard in the inflection in his voice, the things he hadn't put into words. Things that made it suddenly harder for her to breathe.

But his body language was relaxed, as if he'd come to a decision of sorts. She wanted to know what it was. Knew it was probably nothing at all—just her overactive imagination and his exhaustion.

So she remained silent as well. The tree lights danced and the scent of spruce filled the air. The candles on the tree reflected off the packages beneath, giving a festive sparkle to the foil wrappings and glittery bows. The *Nutcracker Suite* played in the background on the CD player Brooke had placed there, knowing, believing no one would ever steal it.

Or it played until the CD stopped. Brooke started to get up.

"Wait," Duncan said. "I'll get it."

The music started again minutes later, a beautiful, jazzy Christmas selection, played by a strong clarinet and gentle flute. Brooke watched Duncan finish with the stereo settings, then return to where she sat. This time he sat closer, draped his arm on the back of the bench and looked her in the eyes.

She grew a little dizzy from what she saw there.

"I'm sorry," he said. "But what with you and Nettie in ER this morning and the hellacious day I had after, it was late when I remembered." He looked down at her lap, reached over and toyed with the hem of her romper. "This CD is the best I could do for eleven pipers piping."

The gifts. It had been Duncan all this time. It had been Duncan! "Why?" was all she could ask. And she barely managed that one word with her heart in her throat, the ache so fierce that she couldn't even swallow.

"Long story. I'll tell you another time. But the main reason is because I wanted to. As much as I wanted to avoid Christmas this year, I saw what it meant to you. I liked seeing that. I wanted to see that." He looked up then. "I needed, Brooke, to see that."

"Why?" she mouthed again. This time not even a whisper of air could escape the constriction of her throat. Her chest burned. Her heart thump-thumped. "Why didn't you tell me? Because you didn't know what to say? What to ask for?"

"No," he said. "Because, until today, I didn't know."

She closed her eyes. Tried to take a deep breath before she read too much into what he was saying. Although what he was saying was so clear she didn't know if she'd ever be able to breathe again.

Still, she wanted him to make it clearer. "What are you saying, Duncan?"

His hand was warm where it caressed her knee. "I'm saying that I've watched you, seen the way you give to your friends. The way you give so much of yourself. The way you feel. You make me want to feel."

The last of her protective resistance melted. An adoring puddle at his feet, she murmured, "Oh, Duncan. It's so easy. All you have to do is open your heart. To know that it's okay to be afraid. To know that with time, with care, hurt will heal."

The lobby clock tolled midnight and Brooke smiled. It was Christmas.

"Can you give me that?" he asked, and with a smile, added, "For Christmas?"

"Christmas is only a start, Duncan. It'll take longer than one day."

"I want longer than one day, Brooke." The candlelight shone bright in his eyes. "I want to hear you sing in the shower. I want to eat your shortbread cookies until I'm sick. I want to watch you while you watch the ballet, while you listen to the music. Watch you watch me when you think I'm not looking."

"What are you saying?"

"I'm saying that letting you into my life is worth any risk to my heart because shutting you out will kill me. I'm saying that I love you, Brooke Bailey."

He took her hand then, pressed it to his chest, covered her fingers with his own. "Do you feel that?" he asked, and she nodded as his heart pumped madly against her palm. "This is my gift for day twelve."

Twelve drummers drumming. The tears that had welled earlier spilled from her eyes. "It's enough, Duncan. It's more than enough."

And then he pulled her close and kissed her lips gently, tenderly, touching the tip of his tongue to hers in the barest sharing of intimacy. When he finally raised his head, a vulnerable question lurked in his frowning gaze.

"I love you, too—" her fingertip smoothed his brow "—Dr. Grinch," she added teasingly. "It might take years to improve your bedside manner, but I'm willing to practice if you are."

Her smile fading, she took his palm, laid it over her breast so he could feel her heart.

It beat to the same drummer as his.

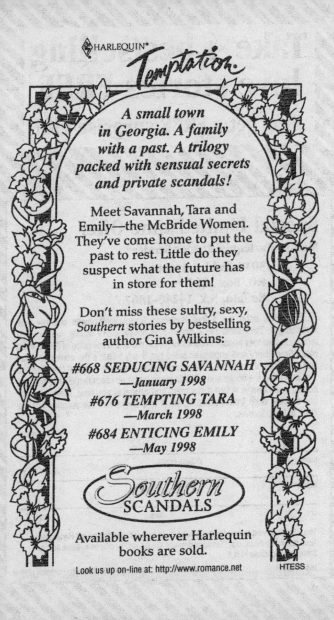

Take 4 bestselling love stories FREE
Plus get a FREE surprise gift!

It's hot...
and it's out of control!

BLAZE

This January, Temptation turns up the
heat. Look for these bold, provocative,
ultra-sexy books!

NIGHT HEAT
by Lyn Ellis

Tripp Anderson had been hired to protect
beautiful, sexy, *rich* Abby Duncan. Keeping his
gorgeous client safe wasn't hard—keeping his
hands off her *was*. But when Abby was threatened,
Tripp vowed to look after her, even if it meant
keeping watch day and night. Little did he expect
his night *watch* to become night *heat*....

BLAZE! Red-hot reads from Temptation!

HARLEQUIN® *Temptation*

THE MEN OF BACHELOR CREEK

Alaska. A place where men could be men—and women were scarce!

To Tanner, Joe and Hawk, Alaska was the final frontier. They'd gone to the ends of the earth to flee the one thing they all feared—MATRIMONY. Little did they know that three intrepid heroines would brave the wilds to "save" them from their lonely bachelor existences.

Enjoy

**#662 CAUGHT UNDER
THE MISTLETOE!**
December 1997

#670 DODGING CUPID'S ARROW!
February 1998

#678 STRUCK BY SPRING FEVER!
April 1998

by Kate Hoffmann

Available wherever Harlequin books are sold.

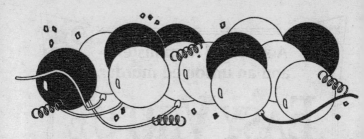

Ring in the New Year with

New Year's Resolution:

FAMILY

This heartwarming collection of three contemporary stories rings in the New Year with babies, families and the best of holiday romance.

Add a dash of romance to your holiday celebrations with this exciting new collection, featuring bestselling authors **Barbara Bretton, Anne McAllister** and **Leandra Logan.**

Available in December,
wherever Harlequin books are sold.

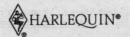

HARLEQUIN WOMEN KNOW ROMANCE WHEN THEY SEE IT.

Free Gift Offer

With a Free Gift proof-of-purchase
from any Harlequin® book, you can receive
a beautiful cubic zirconia pendant.

This stunning marquise-shaped stone is a genuine cubic
zirconia—accented by an 18" gold tone necklace.
(Approximate retail value $19.95)

Send for yours today...
compliments of ◈ HARLEQUIN®

To receive your free gift, a cubic zirconia pendant, send us one original proof-of-purchase, photocopies not accepted, from the back of any Harlequin Romance®, Harlequin Presents®, Harlequin Temptation®, Harlequin Superromance®, Harlequin Intrigue®, Harlequin American Romance®, or Harlequin Historicals® title available at your favorite retail outlet, together with the Free Gift Certificate, plus a check or money order for $1.65 U.S./$2.15 CAN. (do not send cash) to cover postage and handling, payable to Harlequin Free Gift Offer. We will send you the specified gift. Allow 6 to 8 weeks for delivery. Offer good until December 31, 1997, or while quantities last. Offer valid in the U.S. and Canada only.

Free Gift Certificate

Name: _____

Address: _____

City: _____ State/Province: _____ Zip/Postal Code: _____

Mail this certificate, one proof-of-purchase and a check or money order for postage and handling to: HARLEQUIN FREE GIFT OFFER 1997. In the U.S.: 3010 Walden Avenue, P.O. Box 9071, Buffalo NY 14269-9057. In Canada: P.O. Box 604, Fort Erie, Ontario L2Z 5X3.

FREE GIFT OFFER   084-KEZ

ONE PROOF-OF-PURCHASE
To collect your fabulous FREE GIFT, a cubic zirconia pendant, you must include this
original proof-of-purchase for each gift with the properly completed Free Gift Certificate.

084-KEZR